Dempsey Gray grew up in Sharjah, UAE and has since lived in Andorra, France and Spain. She and her husband Martin live with their rescued pet Terrapin, Terry, who dominates the garden near Chichester, West Sussex. With a love of travel, particularly Latin America, she takes every opportunity to meet people, enjoy local food, wine, culture and scenery of all new places she travels to. She speaks French and Spanish and is a qualified soft tissue therapist.

To the memory of my wonderful, funny and loving mother, who was beautiful on the inside and out. Thank you for being my mum.

I am writing this story in the names of my grandmothers, Agnes Dempsey and Mable Gray. This is my tribute to you both, two women who I never knew which is my loss, but by all accounts, you were fantastic, strong and caring women.

To Dad for just being you and my dad, you will never understand the word "No" and you do everything your way, a credit to you.

To Cheri, I don't know how it happened, but thank you from the bottom of my heart for picking us all up, dusting us off and for helping each of us deal with the reality of life with dementia and for being a delightful friend with such a zest for life.

To Maddie and Rou, for your wonderful friendship, you never asked but always listened. Both of your fiendish senses of humour are a joy!

Mandi and Sarah, two more bubbly cousins there will never be, your thoughtful help made our own troubles easier to bear.
To everyone at the Old Malthouse and Sussex Grange, thank you for taking such good care of my mum and for always smiling and saying hello, even in the bleakest of moments.

MAJ, for always being there, whiskey in hand.

Matias, Alejo, Ezequiel and Fernando, for your love, enthusiasm and passion for your country, which first put Argentina on my radar. To all of my Argentinian friends, you all have such a tremendous sense of who you are.

To everyone who I have ever met along this journey called life, who has offered me love, kindness, friendship, guidance and wisdom. Sheila, I've never forgotten your three golden uses for men!

Finally Martin, thank you for putting up with everything, your never-ending love, good sense and support and for all of the fun and adventures and the moments when you make me laugh so much, I can't breathe! I'd be utterly lost without you. I love you so much.

Dempsey Gray

REFUGE IN THE LAND OF SILVER

AUSTIN MACAULEY PUBLISHERS™

LONDON • CAMBRIDGE • NEW YORK • SHARJAH

A CIP catalogue record for this title is available from the British Library.

ISBN 9781398431935 (Paperback)
ISBN 9781398431942 (ePub e-book)

www.austinmacauley.com

First Published 2022
Austin Macauley Publishers Ltd®
1 Canada Square
Canary Wharf
London
E14 5AA

Helen Lawless, for the early day edits and recommendations.

Aimee Ellery, to the sensitive description and sharing your feelings at Auschwitz.

To the many people who have in one way or another worked to make this story to come life.

I felt suddenly bereft of friends, bereft of everything, as desolate and lonely as a man could be.
The Long Walk by Slavomir Rawicz
Poco a poco, se anda lejos – little by little, one walks far
Peruvian Proverb

I remember that we would talk about going horseback riding in the hills through the vineyards. If I closed my eyes, I would be able to feel the sun on my face and hear the bees and insects in the wild flowers around us. The streams would be running fast from the meltwater that came down from the majestic mountains, that framed the backdrop of our surroundings and I would look up to the skies and see the famous birds of prey soaring overhead. I was surrounded by excited female chatter and laughter and I would feel complete and utter peace and happiness and know in that moment that I was in my spiritual home with those who I loved best. The aroma of the meat cooking over the fire and the satisfying richness of the red, full-bodied wine added to the pleasure of the moment. This was my moment, a moment that offered me sanctuary from my circumstances and where I knew I truly belonged.

Bates, Bell, Buss, Cooper, Dexter, Langridge, Lenham, Oakman, Parks, Shaw, Suttle and Thomson—The West Sussex Cricket Team, who defeated the West Indies at Hove Cricket Ground on 12 September 1963

12 January – 2016 –12st 6 – BP 120/60 – RHR 60 b/min

I wish to monitor my own decline, and for those who are interested, this may offer some medical information regarding the onslaught and progression of my condition. The names of my beloved team mates will be my own little test to see just how long I can remember them all for.

My name is James John McCarthy. I'm writing this because of a series of events that have occurred recently and I want to write this while I can. I know from experience with others that now is the time to do this because tomorrow does come and then it is too late. I don't know how long I will be able to write this for, to remember and articulate this story as it truly was, the details of it are key as they are a part of what so captured my attention. It's a story that I don't want to ever forget but the reality is that one day, sooner or later, I will. Hopefully, when that happens, there will be someone who can read this back to me and maybe I will remember if not exactly, perhaps, the essence of the story. Failing that, then there is a chance I will still be intrigued and enjoy what I now have to say.

I hope I will see the telling of this story out and should ever anyone read this later when I am gone, perhaps it will intrigue them as it has me over the years and impart in them the zeal to learn and know more about the history of others and its subsequent effects on their descendants and in turn how they have dealt and continue to deal with the consequences of their forefathers' actions.

I've recently retired from my role as a GP in the village where I have lived for the last 40 or so years. I moved here after the break down of my marriage; an event that shook my whole world and left me bewildered and lacking in confidence. However, I quickly settled into my new environment and with a new rhythm and beat to my life that allowed me to bury my hurt and loose myself in the daily concerns of my new community, I forged forwards. I enjoyed my position and standing within the village and although my status changed professionally the day I ceased to work, I'm still someone respected and sort after for my opinion on all matters arising from rashes to stomach pains, to new-born's names and the best type of washing powder to stop itching. I have an intimate knowledge of the wellbeing and health of all members of my West Sussex village and the surrounding areas. I've guided a fair few of them from birth into adulthood, overseen their childhood illnesses, broken bones, introduction to contraception through to parenthood with the ensuing stresses and strains, insomnia, fatigue, depression and lack of self-esteem. In some cases, the breakdown of relationships as a result of the most natural of all events in the animal world. I have shared in the delight of bringing new life into the world and the pure joy of the magical moments of the first steps on the road to a life time of events ahead. At the other end of the spectrum, I've watched and stood by responsible, upright members of society go through their working life to retirement with bad backs, arthritis and the inevitable downward plunge to the blights of old age. I've supported my patients through these trials, the side effects of their treatments, their fears with facing their own mortality and then the sad but inevitable devastation of their loved ones coping and coming to terms with their loss, some more successfully than others.

There are few aspects of the human life with which I am not familiar. The cycle of life in a happy, safe, relatively affluent, close knit society has no surprises for me. Therefore, this is why I want to tell my future me this story, because it was so different and it challenged my safe compliant world within which I knew all the answers and was entirely confident.

I was born in 1943 in County Cork, Ireland. My father was a psychiatrist and my mother a ward sister. We moved to England in 1945 where I had a happy childhood. The only real irritation to my world was my older brother, Denis. I was by far and in a way more gifted, funny and intelligent of the two of us, however, he always seemed to go one better on all fronts. I felt that he stole my limelight and as a result we were compared, I had to work more at my "brilliance" than perhaps I should have had to.

I was the apple of my parent's eye, born two years after the cot death of my sister, Iona. Named incidentally after the monastery in Scotland, where the Book of Kells was lovingly produced. My father had been a fellow at Trinity College, Dublin or to give it its proper name, The College of the Holy and Undivided Trinity of Queen Elizabeth near Dublin and this great school of learning, instigated by Queen Elizabeth I, now houses the most holy of all books in Ireland. Such is its importance that not a single book published in England, Ireland or the whole British Isles does not get sent to Trinity College for them to hold a copy.

The only time I ever encountered anything other than complete love and adoration was from an aunt. I recall in later years Aunt Bridget (who from that moment on, I despised), telling me that I was a spoilt brat as a result of my parents over compensating and giving me everything after Iona's cot death. Clearly, she didn't know what she was talking about as I was naturally a superior being and she was sour and jealous of my natural attributes. I was brilliant at school, taking all of my exams at least a year ahead of my age group. I was a gifted sportsman, a good looking, a cheeky chap with a lively wit and humour and the ability to charm the birds from the trees. I always got what I wanted and there were few who did not fall for my charms. I could, one way or another, persuade anyone to do anything for me. My future was set to be golden. Not only did I get into Guys Medical School on a full scholarship but I was picked to play for Sussex and was destined to be part of the squad against the West Indies in the 1963 game (which if you know anything about cricket and are interested in its history, you will know that that game was something very special.). Really my life was rather good.

Bates, Bell, Buss, Cooper, Dexter, Langridge, Lenham, Oakman, Parks, Shaw, Suttle and Thomson

14 January – 2016 – 12st 6 – BP 120/60 – RHR 59 b/min

I regained consciousness after three weeks in a coma. I don't remember anything of the events of the night that led up to the car crash. I was driving and Stanley, my best mate, who was in the passenger seat was killed outright. Charges were never brought against me as there were no witnesses and the police could not decide who or what was responsible for the car accident with what was left of it. That was a complete write off and there was little evidence to be had. It was months before I left hospital. My back was broken and I had to learn to walk again. Obviously, my cricket career was finished. I had to repeat a year of study at Guys. The year before I was a daemon, from then on, I was a pitied shambles. Slowly I regained my shattered confidence but I was a shadow of who I had been.

My brother, Denis, is seven years my senior and his career at Guys was one of glory, playboy antics and sporting greatness. He went into dentistry and played to a very high level of amateur golf. Whatever he did, he excelled at.

However, I had been set to be even better in my field before my accident.

I didn't make the 12, who took the West Indies to task, on 12 September 1963, however, each and every one of them came to visit me on my path to recovery and the captain brought me the trophy to admire after their sensational victory. I was touched more than I cared to acknowledge when I received a letter signed by the whole team, dedicating their win to me and they enclosed a small replica trophy with all of their names engraved on it, together with the date of the match. Between Lenham and Oakman was the name McCarthy. It is a small cup with a lid and that letter lives in the bowl of the cup, safely out of view with the lid over it. To this day, that trophy reminds me of who I really am and how admired I was. It was my prized possession; occasionally, it makes me sad that I no longer have it but I feel no remorse about its departure from my world. The fact that I even had it has given me all the recognition that I ever needed.

My brother visited intermittently but was always on his way to another golf tournament and to my mind talked incessantly about a sport for which I had no interest as in my eyes, golf had none of the grace and brilliance of cricket. My view for which I make no apologies was and still is that cricket was a game of the intellectually as well as physically gifted and golf was for those who had nothing better to do. Cricket was a game for those who enjoyed playing at another level rather than merely just playing a sport. He went on to be a highly successful dental surgeon, a revered amateur golfer, who then married a beautiful, funny, intelligent lady and together they took off to the Middle-East to work tax free and escape the bureaucracy of the NHS. To my mind, he sold out but with this came relief as he was then out of my world, though by that stage my world wasn't what it once was and should have been.

Regardless my own route forwards and although I faced some setbacks, I still did pretty well. I may not have played in that glorious match and subsequent Sussex matches but I qualified well and had a fulfilling career with several papers published and well-received. A few inferior and petty fellow professions took issue with some of my views, branding me puritanical and pompous on my views about needless calories and declining exercise, views which I hasten to point out, I have sadly been proved right about since.

Bates, Bell, Buss, Cooper, Dexter, Langridge, Lenham, Oakman, Parks, Shaw, Suttle and Thomson

21 January – 2016 –12st 6 – BP 130/60 – RHR 61 b/min

Following my accident, the lovely Elizabeth, a fellow medical student, visited me regularly and managed to keep my spirits from plummeting completely and a couple of years after we had finished our rotations and were doctors accepted into local practices, we celebrated our success by marrying.

Thinking back, I couldn't offer Lizzie much of a marriage; she loved people and fun and parties. An outgoing and energetic person, she wanted me to be as involved and as enthusiastic as she was in all aspects of our lives together. I was happy watching the cricket and I played a little but mainly I was at my happiest with the papers and my books. Since my accident, my appetite for social gatherings and idiotic chatter along with pointless pleasantries and false interest had rather vanished.

Parties bored and frankly appalled me. People talk such drivel and a couple of drinks will see the most articulate of people making inane and thoughtless remarks, to which all around will laugh as if it's the funniest of jokes they have ever heard. When you question them or point out the stupidity of their comments, everyone gets embarrassed, won't make eye contact with you and then magically disburse and before you know it, you have a reputation for being offensive and rude. We left more than one party under a cloud and Lizzie refusing to speak to me for days on end. Such events left me feeling fractious and irritable. I grew to hate large groups of people and walking into a crowded room brought me out in a cold sweat. I could feel my blood pressure rising and hear the blood pounding in my ears rather like it does just before you faint. Looking into a room of faces, I would find my vision would become blurred as there were too many details to take on board in one go. I would frequently either find the nearest chair and sit down, not speaking to anyone or simply and more commonly turn around and walk back out.

Coupled with the stresses of long working hours and little money, it wasn't too long before our differences became hideously apparent and no matter how deeply I loved her, I didn't meet Lizzie's expectations as a husband. I suppose looking back, at this time I should have stepped up and tried to fix my marriage. My pride and a refusal to accept blame of any sort meant that our home wasn't very loving or even really that pleasant I now realise.

It utterly destroyed me and broke my heart, causing me more pain than 70 broken backs and such a sense of loss and devastation when nine years into our marriage, one day the strain became too much and Lizzie packed her suitcase, informing me that she was leaving me and moving in with one of the senior partners in my practice. I remember watching her as she packed and hearing her speak, her voice getting shriller and shriller as she tried not to cry. I couldn't hear the words she uttered and the whole event seemed bizarre, rather like a dream.

The whole scene took on a surreal quality.

I didn't try to stop her and just stared as she picked up her belongings and bag and turned to look at me. There was a strange look on her face as we stared at each other in silence, reflecting on that moment, it was, I suppose, a look of hopeful desperation, yet I didn't grasp that at the time, so shocked was I by what was happening to my world. Slowly she turned her head towards the door and walked out. As I watched her walk down the road, I could see her shoulders heaving. It never once occurred to me to reach out to her, offer her some comfort, try to broker a deal of reconciliation and make promises to change my ways or plead for our future. Thinking back to the look she gave me before she walked away, there was a sense of pleading in her eyes, perhaps she had been hoping I would in some way offer her reassurance, promise to be somebody else or even just to fight for our future together. I never did and that sealed the end of my marriage to a woman who did more for me at a time that I needed help than I ever realised and who I repaid with sulky bitterness and behaviour boarding on offensive.

The pain and humiliation of Lizzie's departure were so profound that I handed in my notice the very next day and without a job to go to, left Brighton and moved in with a friend. Fortune favours the brave they say. I was far from brave at this time, in fact, years later my very good friend from medical school, Frank, told me I was a miserable bastard and unbearable to be around, more so than normal. However, in a remote and what seemed like a somewhat incestuous, parochial village in West Sussex that bordered on the

Hampshire boundary, an overweight, jovial and port loving Dr Britton had a massive stroke and from my point of view, conveniently popped his clogs and the job of village doctor together with accommodation over the practice became mine.

Bates, Bell, Buss, Cooper, Dexter, Langridge, Lenham, Oakman, Parks, Shaw, Suttle and Thomson

26 January – 2016 –12st 6 – BP 122/60 – RHR 58 b/min

A few months ago, I had a bit of a fall. I went down on my knees and my head smacked against the edge of the tall boy in my bedroom. I ended up with bloody stains on the carpet and butterfly stitches to my eyebrow and a black eye, a silly careless accident soon forgotten. The second fall was caused by standing up too quickly and feeling dizzy. I had several incidents whereby I walked into a room to do something and couldn't remember what. I found that I was starting sentences, which I couldn't finish because I couldn't remember what I had been saying or I would forget the most obvious of words. I'd find myself going somewhere in the village and then wonder why and how I got there. Last month, I woke up from a snooze while in my armchair, the paper was on my lap and the news on the TV had been replaced with some ghastly daytime reality chat show, where people feel the necessity to reveal their most private and intimate of problems to the nation. Once I had come too and my eyes had adjusted to the light, I became aware that there was a woman standing watching me in the corner of the room. I wasn't sure who she was but felt entirely at ease with her presence and looked for another channel to watch. I forgot she was there and it was only after a little while I realised I had ignored her and hadn't offered her a chair. When I looked round at her, she had disappeared, obviously offended by my rudeness.

The following day, I got myself ready and set out to the village to get the paper. To my surprise, I found myself in one of the ploughed fields surrounding the village and talking to this same woman. I asked her why she had walked out on me the day before, again she suddenly vanished and I found myself looking at thin air in the middle of a muddy field. I realised then it was time and I could hear the clock starting to tick, I had to write my story. I know that medicine can't help me and I am following the same path of some of my most beloved patients who I had stood by over the course of my professional life. It is time to take steps to ease my future. I know what my fate holds in store for me and I feel rather indifferent to it. I will face it with all the dignity and courage I can muster but ultimately, I know I will not win the war, just maybe though I may be victorious in one or two small battles, this is the best I can hope for. I must remember to call my solicitor and ensure that I have a power of attorney set up and my will is up to date. I also need to consult with my accountant and measures will need to be taken.

Bates, Bell, Buss, Cooper, Dexter, Langridge, Lenham, Oakman, Parks, Shaw, Suttle and Thomson

3 February – 2016 – 12st 4 – BP 117/72 – RHR 68 b/min

I was quite inflexible about some things and one of those was my morning cup of coffee. Donatella's coffee shop in the high street had been owned by the Petrucci family from Naples for many years and their coffee was in a class of its own. I would start my morning surgery at 8.30 am for the early emergency, vomiting, temperatures and morning after pill appointments. At 11 am, I would take myself to Donatella's for my small black coffee and enjoy 30 minutes of fantastic smells from the Italian cooking and baking, along with frantic and lively chatter. It was one of the most important moments in my day and it made me feel alive, looking in, listening in and in no way being involved in such a chaotic environment. It was like watching a soap opera with three dimensions and smells added in for special effect. It was the perfect solution to my aversion to gatherings of people. I could analyse all that was going on without actually having to be any part of it.

Many had tried to engage me in mindless chatter over the years but slowly came to respect that this was my time and eventually left me alone to enjoy my coffee. At 11.30, I would reluctantly leave the safe, warm and familiar haven of Donatella's and immerse myself in two hours of house visits to those who could not make it to see me. It was a rhythm that suited me well and one that I cherished dearly.

My afternoons were as any other GP's would be, with my surgery running on until at times 7 pm. I struggled to keep to the time allotted by the NHS to each appointment and frequently overran. My patients never complained as they knew that when they saw me, I would give them the time that they needed. I prided myself on giving my patients their time and listening to them, both the things that they said and listening out for what was not said. Being my own boss as it were, it was a luxury not available to so many of my colleagues throughout the country.

I was happy to work as late as I needed to and when I was finished, I would turn off all the lights and go upstairs to find whatever was in the fridge and absentmindedly eat while reading the papers, watching the news and sport and then dive into my books on philosophy. I was frequently still reading at 2 am and more often than I care to admit, I woke in the early hours with my book in my lap and a sore neck. I had built myself a happy cocoon and I believed for many years that I was satisfied with my life.

More from guilt, I suspect, born from doing the dirty on me, Lizzie would periodically turn up to visit and take me to task on the piles of papers stacked in the corner, the dust on the mantel piece, the grimy windows, the three month out of date pre-packaged food in the fridge, my shabby and in her opinion "frankly hobo like" appearance.

'And, my God, please, have a shave and haircut.'

'Do you even know how to work a washing machine?' It seemed easier to make her shut up than endure these less and less frequent but increasingly more poisonous rants, so I engaged Mrs Miller to come in a couple of times a week and clean my flat, put my washing on, make and change my bed, do my shopping and throw out anything from my fridge which was in danger of being classified as pre-historic.

She kindly would leave me notes, telling me when I had to present myself at the barbers and we had an agreement, she could throw out the pile of papers on the left hand side of the door as you came into my living room but the ones on the right were to be left strictly alone. There was a lot of distrust from both parties regarding my papers and I suspect that she threw away some of the supplements that I hadn't yet got round to reading while I overheard her telling Sarah, my secretary, that she thought I was pinching back papers that I had left on the bin pile. I was, but only occasionally, as sometimes you need to refresh your memory or don't recall all of the facts from an article previously read. Still we rubbed along with only a few grumbles. The first time Lizzie came to check up on me after Mrs Miller had started, it was a very uncomfortable and stilted visit as there really was nothing for her to bitch and gripe about, everything was clean and tidy and I was looking "more respectable at long last". Though, apparently, my linen suit made me look more like "a sad, washed up, Florida expat". Eventually, Lizzie ceased to visit at all, a fact that made me equally sad and relieved.

I still loved her more than I can even begin to describe but she was clearly still so angry with me and would vent this rage in a caustic manner which I found demeaning and draining. She was less and less of the woman I remembered and I noticed some very harsh, pinched lines around her mouth that I didn't recall being there when we married. They made her look very bitter and disapproving. Had I done that? Marred her clear and smooth face? The last time she came, she talked incessantly about her "marvellous" jewels and designer dresses from her now husband, fantastic friends, who had race horses, with whom they did lunch and went on boozy jaunts to The Rivera in open topped sports cars. The holidays to the Caribbean and soirees at the opera and theatre, followed by late night dinners of dishes with names I couldn't pronounce and have no idea what they were, frankly left me shuddering and dismayed that one who I loved so much was so taken in by what in my view was such a shallow and meaningless existence.

Where was the wonderful girl I had fallen in love with and still was in love with, who was dedicated to medicine and helping the sick to be well. Who had such noble principals and was full of compassion, who didn't give a seconds thought to making her own clothes and wearing second hand castoffs. Who, happily, ate fish and chips out of newspaper and who would stay up arguing with me all night over principals and philosophical points? Who laughed as much as she loved, where on earth did she go? Maybe she was still there but I just couldn't see her, maybe she was still there but seeing me made her change into this new defensive and slightly hostile pretentious woman. Maybe I had rose tinted glasses on and was holding onto a romantic and now historical image.

I shook myself as she got up, as she had to hurry off because her tailor was popping by to take some final measurements for the hunting jacket she was having

28

commissioned. When I enquired if she had taken up hunting, she told me not to be so ridiculous; it was for the drinks party after all "the chaps" had returned from butchering the local wild life. (She might not have said that last bit.) With that, she gave me a final pitting glare and departed with a flourish.

Thinking back, it must have been over 20 years since I last saw her. I get Christmas and birthday cards from her and now text messages informing me if an old school friend has died, re-married or become a grandparent. I rarely bother to respond as I honestly couldn't care less.

Bates, Bell, Buss, Cooper, Dexter, Langridge, Lenham, Oakman, Parks, Suttle and Thomson

13 February – 2016 – 12st 4 – BP 120/72 – RHR 65 b/min

While I worked, I used to go to the pub, The Rose and Crown to watch the cricket highlights with some of the local male folk periodic evenings or on a Saturday or Sunday afternoon. It had become known, I'm not sure how that I had been an excellent cricketer in my former life and this gave me a privileged position with the hardiest of males in the village and my opinion was always sort and my beer always paid for by another. I did try to protest in the early days but eventually, I just gave up but always offered my thanks. I did enjoy these occasions as there was no inane chatter, just measured and well-thought out comments about one of the most skilful and precise of games. Everyone there was enjoying the moment and the ease of male companionship, a kindred passion and appreciation of a beautiful game.

It's easy to see how so many years slipped by and I don't regret any of them as they held a comfortable peace for me. When I retired, a couple of female general practitioners, who had young families shared my practice between them on a part time basis. It worked well and I enjoyed being upstairs with my papers listening to the hum of the practice below and from time to time, I would make guest appearances in the waiting room to chat to some of my favourite, now former patients. More than once, I had to cover last minute emergencies when Tanya and Lisa couldn't make it to work on time if at all as a result of the strains of a young family. I would grumble to them but secretly, I was thrilled as I was still needed. Being able to save the day always gave me a little ego boost. The village had grown in the years I was there and more and more of the outlying areas were no longer under our practice but under the jurisdiction of the larger towns slightly further afield, still we retained our healthy client base numbers and it took considerable strain off us as a practice that we no longer had to travel any real distance to see our patients, as they were now all local to the village which was fast becoming a small town.

You now have an idea about my life, who I was and how I felt about it.

Bates, Bell, Buss, Cooper, Dexter, Langridge, Lenham, Oakman, Parks, Shaw, Suttle and Thomson

14 February – 2016 – 12st 4 – BP 120/60 – RHR 62 b/min

Now let me tell you my story, which began in mid to late March 1995.

One cold and miserable day, I walked into Donatella's for my morning coffee and without looking at the young waitress, I said, 'My usual, please.' It had been raining heavily outside and I was trying to avoid getting my clothes wet while taking off my dripping mac.

'And what would your usual be please?' I looked up sharply; a little miffed that she hadn't recognised me from the day before and all the days before that, only it was a face I had never seen before smiling back at me.

'Who are you?' I demanded slightly on the back foot, this was a break from an established routine.

'*Hola*, I am Lorena, who are you? And what is your usual please?' At this point, old Donatella herself bustled forward in her ample matronly manner.

'Doctor, Doctor, (in Italian) I'm so sorry! (English) She is a new girl, my cousin's daughter, she is learning. Leave this to me, I promise this will never happen again!' And with that, the new girl, Lorena, Donatella's cousin's daughter, was shoved from my sight to the sound of hysterical shouting and yelling. A sound which had long since failed to alarm me, as I soon came to realise that this is how you have a conversation where there is any Italian involved.

I had often sat and contemplated while drinking my coffee, why Donatella was so plump as she waved her arms around so much and used up so much energy just speaking; she should, by rights, have been as lean as a whippet. The mouth-watering smells emulating from her kitchen were undoubtedly the answer.

The next morning at coffee time, I met Lorena again. This time she greeted me with the same beaming smile and said,

'*Hola*, Doctor, how are you today? A small black coffee right away.' With that she spun around on her heel not waiting for an answer as she had clearly been told to not converse with me more than was strictly necessary and returned a few moments later with my coffee. She had obviously read the rule book or had been threatened with death, possibly both, because for the next couple of weeks, she would always welcome me in the same way and then leave me well alone to my coffee.

One morning due to a mix up and last minute cancellation, I found that I had a bit longer in the coffee shop to savour my small black coffee. No one else was in the coffee shop, just Lorena and I. Feeling remarkably cheerful and chatty, when Lorena brought my coffee to me, I looked up to her and asked her if she would like to join me. She looked around the cafe and let out a big and slightly exaggerated sigh.

'Oh, Doctor, I have so many people to attend to but I cannot.' She could have just said no thank you and I did feel a little rejected. I then looked at her to discover that she was laughing at me and with a flourish pulled out a chair and said,

'Come on, let's talk!'

Instantly I didn't know what to say but I need not have worried as she seemed to have more than enough to say for the both of us.

As I watched her, wondering at what point she would pass out through lack of breath, I noted that she had the most glorious, thick, glossy black hair, which was well down her back. It really did look like liquid silk, which I realise is a silly thing to say as there is no such thing; just one of those ridiculous sayings that is overused and is pointless but somehow seemed to sum up her crowning glory. Her thick lashed dark eyes seemed to dance with light and her deep smile added a beauty to her face, which it may not have naturally have had. She oozed health and vitality in a way that only the young can do.

She told me that she was the middle of three children and was in her early 20s. Her family was from a place called Mendoza in the Andes Mountains that failed to register with me. She had qualified as a physiotherapist just before Christmas, which is the southern hemisphere's summer and had come to Europe for our winter to teach skiing in a Pyrenean resort. This was ideal for her as she could teach in her native Spanish and make some new friends and have fun after so many years of intense study.

'You are thinking, an Argentinean in England, I am mad, no?' I wasn't, I was starting to think that people in the southern hemisphere must have abnormally large lungs.

'But you guys don't seem to mind me here, so I can practice my English.'

'Excuse me, but why should we mind you being here?' I queried.

'Las Malvinas of cause tonto!' Not having a clue what she had just said, it took me a moment or two to work this out.

'The Falklands?' I queried haltingly. 'Why should we mind we won?' I had finally found the way to halt her in her tracks and I really hadn't intended to. She looked very hurt and offended by this thoughtless comment.

'*Mi tio*, my uncle, he died in this conflict.' I apologised profusely and asked her to carry on telling me about herself. This didn't take too much encouragement and I discovered that the snow season in Europe had been, debil, a word which she flung out with an element of distain, so I concluded that this was an indication of how bad the snow had been. She had arrived here last month after finishing the season early and taking off to Spain and France to travel. Donatella was her father's cousin, several times removed, she tried to explain the relationship to me but it became increasingly complicated as she would refer to each family member by their names and not having a clue who any of these people were, I was lost within seconds. I struggled to understand how the connection could work but thought I would leave that line of questioning for another time. Apparently, it was a given that if she visited, she would have a job. So here she was.

She had wanted to come to England and the opportunity to improve her English should not be wasted, she informed me earnestly. Lorena wanted to spend the summer at Donatella's, visit Stonehenge, Hadrian's Wall and kiss the Blarney Stone and see the Giants Causeway. I couldn't help but notice that there seemed to be a lot of rocks involved here and they were some distance apart. When I mentioned this, she laughed.

'Do you know how big my country is? To visit my grandmother, we had to drive for nearly two days!'

'Anyway, when the summer is over, I will maybe go to Europe for a bit, travel a little and see some sights. I won't see everything but something is better than nothing, don't you think?' Not pausing for breath much less a response, she bounded on.

'It is so very interesting to visit different countries and meet different people to see how they live and understand their customs and culture, don't you think?' Her questions never seemed to actually need answers. 'It makes you see the world in a bigger way.'

'A broader context,' I quietly corrected her, seizing the first opportunity I had had to speak for a few moments.

At this point the bell above the door rang and a mother with a pushchair and small child who was crying came in. The bubble was burst and I hurried out realising I was going to be late for my visit.

Bates, Bell, Buss, Cooper, Dexter, Langridge, Lenham, Oakman, Parks, Shaw, Suttle and Thomson

6 March – 12st 4 – BP 110/75 – RHR 75 b/min
Early April 1995

I didn't have much time to reflect on our conversation until the end of my day. After dinner, I found my old atlas and encyclopaedia which I confess I hadn't picked up in many years; the internet was not yet a common household appliance so, yes, it was these books which I consulted and found out exactly where Argentina was.

I had a vague idea but didn't know that it was the eighth largest country in the world and the second largest in South America, piped to the post by Brazil, which is the fifth largest worldwide, in real terms Argentina is less than one-third the size of the United States, which is the third largest in the world. Bordered by Chile to the West and Brazil and Bolivia to the North as well as Paraguay and Uruguay, an area 6,005 miles of land boundaries and 3,100 miles of coastline, Argentina is the largest Spanish-speaking nation in the world by area at about 1.07million square miles. A country rich in natural resources being lead, zinc, tin, copper, iron ore, manganese, petroleum and uranium, it's industries voluminous tones informed me are food processing, motor vehicles, consumer durables, textiles, chemicals and petrochemicals, printing, metallurgy and steel. I found myself confronted with pages of facts about agriculture and food production, crops and livestock, wheat production and impressive percentages of this production making the country a strong contender on the world stage. Impressive but utterly uninteresting and not the kind of facts that would ever make a glossy travel brochure. Certainly nothing to really grab the imagination and pip the interest. I remorselessly skipped past these pages.

However, I did feel rather as if I had just discovered a whole new section of the world, which in one regard I suppose I had. My world was predominately a small West Sussex village and the internal wrangling of the NHS. Marginally further afield I was aware of what our government and the opposition were bellyaching about, though nothing new ever seemed to be said. America and the Middle-East periodically sent a shock wave through events and very rarely something heart-warming and positive happened that hit the headlines. That was about as far as my stratosphere went. Beyond that it was all dark matter. I had never considered myself narrow-minded or disinterested, in fact, I am very knowledgeable about a whole range of different subjects, however, I had never really bothered to consider the southern part of the American continent. There had been no real reason to.

As I reflected on this and enjoyed another mouthful of French Cahors very drinkable red wine, I found myself considering what I had just found out. The sheer scale of the land mass, the volume of produce, the agricultural emphasis of this new nation in my world was staggering when one really considered what the statistics meant. I lived in a reasonably rural part of the country. There were fields and livestock. I was aware of the mud from the fields all over the roads from the tractors whenever I went further afield than my little cocoon, which granted wasn't often. I considered what as a nation we produce. Most of it seemed to be done on quotas dictated by some faceless bureaucrat in an office on the continent, who had probably never visited our country. What on earth did that mean for us in the long term? I mused instantly side tracked by this thought. Were we sleep walking into some kind of foreign strangle hold on our nation? I may not have been born English but I considered England to be my country and never once thought of myself as an immigrant.

Casting a look at the clock, it was long past midnight and I had a full day ahead of me tomorrow. My eyes slipped across to my trophy which was next to the ornate mantle clock which I had inherited when my father died. As always when I looked at my trophy, I felt a sense of pride of my worth and it gave me my identity, someone who was really a somebody.

Just as I was about to get into bed, I noticed a bright light from outside the window. I never shut the curtains, in actual fact I couldn't tell you what colour they even were. Walking to my bedroom window to inspect the cause of the light, I realised that it was the moon, big and very bright in the clear sky. Looking at it I thought I could see mountains and craters on it, it was so clear. In that moment, a thought struck me that over millennia, people from all over the world had looked up at this same spectacle and provided we didn't do anything more stupid than we had already done; people from all over the world would look up for many millennia more to marvel at a body that was never changing and which was a fundamental part of our wellbeing and daily life.

Bates, Bell, Cooper, Dexter, Langridge, Lenham, Oakman, Parks, Shaw, Suttle, Thomson and Buss

8 March – 12st 3 – BP 112/65 – RHR 77 b/min
April 1995

I had to forgo my coffee the next day, which made my foul mood even worse. My back had ached terribly and I hadn't been able to get off to sleep until just before my alarm went off. I'd had to deal with a particularly hysterical mother, who had insisted on seeing me without an appointment regardless of what poor Sarah said to her and she had barged her way into my office at the time I would have been getting ready to leave for my coffee. Her frightened child cowered behind his tyrant of a mother. After I asked him what was the matter twice and each time she answered for him, I fixed her with a very frosty glare and informed her that if she did not shut up, I would remove her from the room. The poor child was visibly shaking by this point. A very quick inspection revealed the matter.

'Nits, your son…' I consulted my notes.

'Tyrone?' Honestly, who on earth called their child Tyrone?

'Tyrone has nits. Take this prescription to the pharmacy and see Mrs Bushel behind the counter and get this medicated shampoo and wash your son's hair. Keep him off school until the end of the treatment.'

'He will be fine but we don't want half the county scratching their heads and next time you come barging into my surgery, if you don't have an appointment and if you are as offensive to my secretary again, I will refuse to see you and before you interrupt me again, I find your manner most unpleasant, unfortunately, I cannot prescribe anything for that, though I do recommend judging by your breath that you stop smoking and cut back on the booze. A re-evaluation of your current diet wouldn't go amiss either. Now I am late for my next appointment, goodbye.' I held open the door and shooed this vile woman and her luckless son out.

My day dragged on and I started to wonder if everyone was out to get me. Most of the patients I saw that day were overwrought and incapable of listening to a word I said. I felt distinctly sour and disenchanted with the world when I dragged myself upstairs at the end of the day. On my way back from my last appointment, I had dropped into the Rose and Crown and Shirley behind the bar had poured me a small beer to go with my steak and ale pie. It was warm and cosy in there as it always was but my bad temper was not eased as every mouthful of food that I seemed to take was accompanied by an "Evening Doc" or a "What's up Doc" and a clap on my already desperately aching back. Sullenly, I returned home earlier than I might have otherwise have done.

I sat down in my favourite chair and despondently watched the news, which was about as dismal as my mood. I'd poured myself a rare glass of brandy which I absentmindedly sipped. I didn't often drink spirits but occasional I would indulge myself in a glass of brandy. Lizzie and my father had used to drink whiskey by the bucket load together but it was never a drink that I enjoyed. I recall how they would both get very righteous and would talk through each other, pontificating about whatever subject had captured their attention and at times on entirely different subjects. Sadly, I remember very vividly during one argument between us Lizzie shouting at me saying,

'Why can you not be more like your father? I wish I had never met him because it was his mind and demeanour that I fell in love with and I made the stupid mistake of thinking that you were like him!'

I glanced around and picked up the encyclopaedia again and carried on reading from where I had left off the night before.

I read that the climate in Argentina was mostly temperate, arid in the southeast, sub Antarctic in the southwest, the terrain is varied with rich plains of the Pampas in northern half, (an area subject to Pamperos which are violent windstorms that can strike at certain times) flat to rolling plateau of Patagonia in south, rugged Andes along western border. There are waterfalls of note in the North—The Iguazú Falls, which comprise of over 275 cascades on the border between Brazil and Argentina. The water tumbles over heights of 262 feet and nearly two miles wide. In the South in Patagonia there are glaciers and the Perito Moreno Glacier is the third-largest reserve of fresh water in the world and one of only three glaciers in Patagonia that are growing and not shrinking. The accumulating facts where simply more than I could comprehend. It all seemed rather fantastic and somewhat fascicle. Many thousands of square miles which crossed the international frontier with Chile. Most of which seemed to form part of the Southern Ice Shelf, the third largest mass of ice in the world after Antarctica and Greenland which created and influenced world weather.

I read that it was a country of extremes with the lowest point of the country being Laguna del Carbón, which is a salt lake located in a place called Santa Cruz, at 344 feet below sea level and the highest point being Cerro Aconcagua in the Andes Mountains at 22,835 feet near, I noted, to Mendoza, where young Lorena hailed from and the only place I could now identify with any real confidence. The height of this was unimaginable and I tried to remember what height I had flown at on rare flights to holiday destinations with Lizzie.

The Altitude of the Andes made me breathe in sharply. I also now realised how Lorena could speak without drawing breath. She was used to breathing in zero oxygen air and to come to sea-level must be like an oxygen holiday. Amused by this, I looked up this point in one of my medical books but it seems like I may have exaggerated this point in my mind. I enjoyed the thought though. The distances from one place to another were really quite extraordinary. Other than America or Russia, I could not really imagine going so far and remaining in the same country. A point of interest that I noted is that most people there prefer to use public transport rather than drive cars. I wondered if this was because of the distances involved, maybe cars are expensive there? I'd ask Lorena, not that it really mattered.

I was intrigued to discover that Cerro Aconcagua is one of "The Seven Peaks" of the world and a magnet for climbers as it is considered a non-technical mountain. I wasn't altogether sure what made a mountain technical as the thought of climbing a mountain of any sort seemed arduous. The only mountains which I had ever heard people climbing were generally in the Himalayas and this always seemed to be a rather foolish and ill thought out pastime as more often than not, the expedition invariably seemed to end in disaster and death, which all seemed rather futile and pointless.

I did once read an interesting account of some Italian soldiers, who in 1916 in the north of Italy managed to drag a six tonne 149/G cannon from a village at 3280 feet altitude up an impossibly sheer and steep sided mountain to the summit of Cresta Croce which is at about 10,700 feet. The canon was affectionately called The Hippopotamus. The name speaks for itself as it took many men months to achieve this feat and sadly a number lost their lives to avalanches and misadventure. This was undertaken in impossible conditions in the snow and cold of winter but their gutsy determination prevailed and they were able to anchor the canon to the top of the mountain and bombard the enemy, thus protecting their boarder from the Austrians.

Returning to my book, I continued my education of the facts about the mountains of this part of South America. The Andes is the sixth highest mountain range in the world, the five preceding it are all in Asia. However, it is the longest mountain range in the world running 7000 miles from Colombia to the southern tip of South America in Tierra del Fuego. Apparently, the mountains continue below the level of the sea and carry on to Antarctica. I read that the Andes are a result of plates bearing the ocean crust colliding with the continent of South America.

I did recall a story from some years ago about a rugby team from Uruguay, who had crashed on a flight going over the Andes to Chile, they had nearly all been killed and those who had lived had to survive by eating their dead companions. A far more challenging and complicated task than one may imagine as they would not have had a fully equipped kitchen to prepare their meals, an unfrozen corpse is challenge enough but a frozen one would make this a near impossible task and not to mention the emotional and psychological turmoil and upset. I doubted that many, who read the story, fully appreciated the horrors that those poor people were put though. Possibly a number of those involved never fully appreciated the horrors of what they themselves went through. The mind is remarkably apt at blocking certain horrors or distress, we witness or pain that we feel, so that with time, we cannot recall in detail or with certainty what we have experienced. This is why some people have sudden flash backs years after an event which for the intervening few years, they had no recollection of. Our brains are more extraordinary, then we will ever fully understand.

Taking another sip of brandy, I turned back to my book and was instantly engrossed again my attention fully caught by the unfolding story on the pages before me. Apparently, since the Cretaceous period, about 65 million years ago, the time of the dinosaurs, of which there are more and more significant finds evidencing their presence on this land, the ocean crust has been sliding below the west coast of South America, causing volcanoes and uplift. Indeed two places, one that I had never heard of, San Miguel de Tucuman and the Mendoza area in the Andes subject to earthquakes. So I mused young Lorena lived in an earthquake hotspot. That didn't sound ideal at all.

The Andes are part of the "Rim of Fire" surrounding the Pacific, marked by volcanoes, earthquake zones and deep ocean trenches. The glaciers and snowfields of the Andes supply water to the arid coast of central South America as well as to the Amazon Basin. Swampy, tropical conditions in the very north give way to freezing glacial regions in the south. Patagonia, regarded as one of the most spectacular and dangerous places on the planet, stretches from the southern Andes in the west to the Atlantic Ocean in the east. The southern tip of Argentina known as Cape Horn is one of the stormiest locations there is. Indeed it is an area feared by sailors and tackled only by the intrepid. I must say it did sound most inhospitable there and to find all of that in just one area of a country. Many, I am sure, would argue that in our own country there are many geographical wonders but surely none so extreme? I drifted off to sleep in my chair, aided by fatigue and the warming glow of the brandy.

Bates, Bell, Buss, Cooper, Dexter, Langridge, Menham, Oakman, Parker, Shaw, Suttle and Thomson

9th March – 12st 3 – BP 110/75 – RHR 80 b/min
April 1995

'Doctor, we missed you yesterday. Is all well with you?' The effects of a painful back, a lack of sleep, some undeniably idiotic and rude patients and too much brandy the night before clearly combined to give me a less than glowing complexion and without further ado, Lorena presented me with a very welcome cup of coffee, which seemed rather stronger than usual.

She pulled up a chair and pondered my appearance. 'Shall I tell you some more about my country?' Apparently, given the fact that she didn't wait for a response, she had meant,

'I'm going to take advantage of your fragile state and tell you some more about my country, buckle up.' Within moments, I was transported away to this far away land as she gushed fourth with facts about her homeland. The capital, Buenos Aires, is on the East Coast and is the fourth largest city in the world and Europeans first landed here in 1502. This is where Granny Lorena resided. It is known as the Paris of South America because of its stunning architecture, cosmopolitan atmosphere and love of all of the latest fashions, intimate side walk cafes, not to mention its rich history and ongoing love affair with all of the latest trends. The majestic parks, where friends meet to run and participate in sports, debate with passion, the intricacies of life in the chic and trendy bars and cafes on the periphery of the lakes and rose gardens or just stroll arm in arm enjoying the beauty of the peaceful green haven in a hectic city centre all sounded delightful with their numerous statues and water features.

A spread out city with numerous plazas, many with elaborate and vast fountains in an effort to ease the punishing summer heat, which could frequently hit well into the 30s. Apparently, further north from Mendoza, there is a region in the summer where it was daily into the 40s and sometimes 50s. Though just a couple of hundred miles further South in Mendoza, the winters could be cold and the mountains around the city had ski resorts.

I learnt from a very earnest Lorena that Argentina has a very mixed blood stock. 97% of Argentina's population is home to people of European descent, while 1.5% of people are of Amerindian descent, 0.2% of people are of Asian descent and 1.5% of their population is classified as Mestizos. These are people of mixed heritage. As a nation it has an impressive literacy rate of over 97% and children are required to attend school from ages 5 to 14. The school year in the country begins in March and ends in November. The schooling system is very different to our own, whereby nine years of study are divided into three-year segments. After the nine years, students enter a "multimodal" program that offers general and specialised training.

It is interesting how nations come up with different ideas for education and lifestyle and Lorena went on to tell me that adults and children, both travel home after lunch each day to take a siesta. During siestas, many businesses and schools close down and everyone in the country relaxes. Apparently, there are even a few hotels in the capital city that rent rooms specifically for siestas. By all accounts, though there was a flaw to this as the times and durations of the siestas differed according to which province you reside in due to the climate. In San Juan, for example, the siesta in summer is from 1pm till 6pm and offices will work until past 9pm in an effort to accommodate the hot day time temperatures. However, in Buenos Aires, the siesta is from 1pm until 4pm and offices close at 7pm. As hard as I tried, I could not imagine that working in our culture, though the idea was very attractive. I concluded that as a nation, Argentina was not shrouded in darkness in the winter by 3 pm. Clearly they have more time in their day to rest.

A Roman Catholic country, I was surprised to hear that although the population is 92% Roman Catholic, less than 20% are practicing, while 2% are Protestant, 2% are Jewish and 4% are "other", with a love of the Tango, beef and cowboys or Gauchos as they were known. Before she could take this fascinating anthropology lesson any further, I regretfully stopped her.

'I apologise for interrupting but I must now be on my way, duty calls.'

'I will see you tomorrow and I will be testing you, you know.' She laughed and winked at me before gathering up my cup and swivelling on her heels back to behind the bar. Reluctantly, I went off to take temperatures, listen to chests and prescribe common sense.

I had popped into the corner shop to pay my bill for my papers and I came across a copy of National Geographic. The front cover caught my attention with a title of "Argentina—A land discovered". That night I flicked through my new magazine' there were many glossy photos. The pictures that I found showed 1950s cars and beautiful colonial buildings. There were other photos of suitably macho and serious looking men on horseback, Gauchos with statement hats and elaborate ponchos astride magnificent and highly strung steeds. Lines of vineyards lining the hills and by all accounts, the Mendoza region produced some very drinkable red wine. In fact, I found out that it was quite a major export. I made a mental note to try some.

Bates, Bell, Buss, Cooper, Dexter, Langridge, Lenham, Oakman, Parkinson, Shaw, Suttle and Thomson

4 April – 12st 1 – BP 132/95 – RHR 88 b/min
April 1995

Eager and greedy for more insights into the lovely Lorena's life in a strange and far flung land, I would rush to the café daily when morning surgery was done before my visits, but it was well over a week before I could get my next fix as the café was always busy and Lorena always occupied with coffees and cakes, which she would serve to their clientele. The majority of whom in my view should have been watching their calorific intake and not wasting Lorena's time. Still I had to remind myself that this is a free country and it was good for Donatella's business without which my world would have been a duller place. It did surprise me how quickly I had become absorbed and enthralled by this young woman's world, which was so far removed from my own.

In the intervening evenings, I would read as much as I could about Argentina and its people. In Latin, the meaning of Argentina is silver. The original European settlers believed that the country was full of silver and established towns in the country in order to search for this precious metal. Silver was found here but not in the quantities hoped for and certainly there was no comparison with its neighbour to the north, Bolivia, in the city of Potosi. The highest city in the world at 4,100m and historically the centre of the Spanish Empire's fiscal wealth. Estimates suggest between 1545 until the mid-1990s, 60,000 tons of silver were mined from the mountain which overlooks Potosi, El Cerro Rico (The Rich Mountain). The Spanish Empire's coins were all made at the Royal Mint in Potosi. By the same reckoning, estimates indicate that over eight million lives have been lost due to the appalling mining conditions and the continual use of mercury.

Amerigo Vespucci an Italian explorer, financier, navigator and cartographer is credited with demonstrating that in fact the region collectively known today as South America and the West Indies were independent land masses and not part of Asia as had been assumed by Columbus. On his return to Europe in 1502, Vespucci wrote in a letter to the all-powerful and internationally influential Medici family in Italy explaining that the land masses he had explored were much larger than anticipated and different from the Asia described by Ptolemy or Marco Polo and therefore must be a new world, a previously unknown fourth continent after Europe, Asia, and Africa.

In 1507, Martin Waldseemüller produced an incredible work of the time, Universalis Cosmograpiae, a world map on which he named the new continent 'America' a homophone of Vespucci's first name. His work has proven to be accurate, even by modern standards.

I continued to find out random and interesting facts about this new land. It never occurred to me that possibly the same array of information was available to me about my own homeland equally rich in history, flora and fauna, geographic landmarks, exports and natural resources. Maybe there is some credibility to the saying that you can never see what is in front of you. Or maybe it's never as interesting when it is in front of you and one just takes these things for granted. Who knows and I suppose it doesn't really matter.

Unsurprisingly, for such a large county, there is much fauna and flora and over 10% of the world's flora is found in Argentina. The world's earliest plants were found here, Liverworts, which had no roots or stems, have been dated back to approximately 472 million years ago.

Dinosaurs once roamed this land and some of the evidence of their existence suggests that they were really quite spectacular creatures. Argentinosaurus was one of the biggest known dinosaurs. It was an herbivore named after the country in which it was found and is believed to have been as large 125 feet in length and weighed over 75 tonnes.

Recently, scientists studied how such a large animal was able to walk on land. They scanned the skeleton and reconstructed its movements to study its stride. It turns out these gigantic dinosaurs were able to reach speeds of more than five miles per hour. The oldest predator dinosaur found to date was also discovered here. This oldest carnivore stood on two legs with small arms and big legs called "The Eoraptor". It was a little dog-sized creature, measuring only just over three feet in length. Eoraptor was likely carnivorous, happily feasting on animals 230 million years ago in the northwest of what is now Argentina.

Argentina is apparently the Latin American country that has the most Nobel Prize winners. Five people from Argentina have won Nobel Prizes in the categories of science and peace.

The very first animated film in the world was created by an Argentinean man. Quirino Cristiani created the film 'El Apostol' in 1917. This film was 70 minutes long and had over 58,000 frames.

June 1892, Francisca Rojas's two children were found with multiple stab wounds and undoubtedly the deciding factor to their demise was that their throats had been slit in their rural home in the province of Buenos Aires. She claimed that her neighbour had broken in and committed the terrible and brutal double murder. After days of torture, the neighbour was cleared and declared innocent. A detective from the city was brought in to help with the investigation. Inspector Alvarez looked over the scene of the crime and noticed a bloody fingerprint on the door, which he removed and took for inspection. He proceeded to take Rojas's fingerprints and compared them with the print on the door.

Determining they were a match, Rojas was arrested and there after reluctantly confessed to the horrific crime. Rojas became the first person in the world to be found guilty through fingerprint evidence. Prior to her conviction, an anthropologist, who immigrated to Argentina named Juan Vecutich had begun work on the first filing system for fingerprints. He was a pioneer in fingerprinting evidence and his filing system was the first in the world of its kind. Following on from Rojas's guilty verdict, Argentina became the first country to use fingerprinting as the primary form of identification in criminal records.

Apart from the unpleasant details surrounding the death of these unfortunate children, this story delighted me. It had only been a hundred years ago. Finger printing is now such an accepted and obvious method of identification, yet then it was ground breaking. Who knows what marvels of science we will have revealed 100 years from now. Given our accelerating rate of discovery, the potential is beyond comprehension and our wildest imagination.

I thought back to a brush with the law that I had before my accident. I had an E Type Jaguar at the time, a car that I loved but had to part with, on account of my having to change it in pretty sharpish. I had been accused of ramming into the back of a parked car and driving off without contacting the owners. There were by all accounts some dinks to their bumper and a broken light. Apparently, someone had seen me and reported me. Actually this was entirely true. I had fallen out of a bar with a lovely young blonde and jumping into my car, slightly the worse for wear. I had forgotten that I had left the car in gear. Starting the engine, the car leapt forwards, straight into the car in question. Laughing hysterically, we drove off thinking nothing more of it. When the police came knocking on my door, the next day asking if I owned a green sports car, I effortlessly looked them in the eye and said, 'No, officers, I don't.'

When the door was shut behind them, I waited until they had gone and then retraced my steps from the night before, found my motor and checking that there was no damage, drove to the garage some distance away where I had bought the E Type from and exchanged it for a revved up red mini cooper.

'Watch how you go with this, lad.' The garage owner cautioned me.

'This thing is like shit off a shovel, get it wrong and this thing will eat you alive.'

Stanley died 10 days later on that fateful night that changed my life forever.

Bates, Bell, Buss, Cooper, Dexter, Langridge, Lenham, Oakman, Parkes, Shaw, Suttle and Thomson

7th April – 12st – BP 122/75 – RHR 90 b/min
Late April/Early May 1995

Wandering home after an enjoyable day's work, where I had been introduced to the new and somewhat vocal member of a family, all of whom I had known since they were small babies. I walked home with a feeling of wellbeing. The sun was still shining and the air was filled with the noise of industrious birds going about their business. Not really wanting too much of my own company just yet, I headed in the direction of the bowling green. As I drew near, I could hear the gentle hum of chatter and happy in the knowledge that there was a game still going on that I could watch. I walked down the path and was about to let myself in through the gate to the green when I heard the familiar and slightly husky voice of my young friend.

'Good evening, Doctor, how are you?' Delighted to round my happy day off with the company of such a cheerful companion, I responded that I was very well and asked after her well-being.

'Oh, I'm great. Thank you, Doctor.'

'Shall we watch the game and you can explain the rules to me?'

'I have to confess, Lorena, I'm not an authority on the rules.'

'No problem at all. We will watch and we can guess at them.' She laughed. We sat down on one of the benches, overlooking the green and after some time of intense scrutiny, we both concluded that we didn't really know what was going on.

'We also have some particular sports in my country. Pato, have you heard of Pato?' I wondered if she had mispronounced polo and queried this point.

'No, not polo, P A T O.'

'It is the national sport of Argentina and it means duck. It is a game played on horseback. It is a very fast game and very, very dangerous. The horses gallop from one end of a pitch to another while the riders throw themselves at the "Pato". Before it was a duck but more recently they substituted the duck for a ball, it's better that way, less mess.' Lorena smirked at me and continued, 'The riders often on the ground one side of the galloping horse but still in their stirrups to catch in a small basket the Pato and throw it to another member of the team with the point is to score as many goals which are at either end of the pitch as possible.' It sounded to me a bit like lacrosse on horseback.

'As a nation we are known for winning more international polo championships than any other country in the world. The polo club in Buenos Aires is very grand with elaborate bronze statues celebrating the horse. This is right next to the race track. However, the favourite sport in the country is football. Argentina loves football!' Lorena said, this in a very matter of fact way as if she were reading facts from a book. She continued, 'Football is a game that we take very seriously and there are jealousies that are so deeply rooted between some teams, that violence between fans almost always happens at the games. The big most famous war is between Rio Plate and the Boca Junior team.'

Their rivalry is more of a war between rich and poor. The hatred between the two is very profound and although they are very close to each other in the city, the whole country is influenced by their hatred of each other. Everybody supports one team or the other.

The light was now fast disappearing and the chaps on the green were packing up. A couple of them came up to us to say hello and Lorena leapt at the opportunity to ask Frankie, a well-known personality in the village, all about the rules of the game.

'Fancy a drink, Doc?' Samuel, the local fishmonger asked me.

Seeing the indecision on my face, he said, 'Come on, it will only be a swift half. I've got to be out on the boats in a few hours.' Accepting his offer, I turned and said goodbye to Lorena, who was still engrossed in the complexity of the rules of bowls. Samuel and I enjoyed half-an-hour of discussion about fishing quotas and the recent good weather over a beer.

It was a very lovely end to a very happy day.

Bates, Buss, Cooper, Dexter, Langridge, Lenham, Oakman, Parks, Shaw, Suttle and Thomson

10th April – 12st 1 – BP 120/65 – RHR 64 b/min
Early May 1995

I found myself reading about a whole series of different and random details about topics that usually would have held no interest for me at all. For example, ballroom dancing is an activity that many people apparently partake in on a daily basis. Many ballroom dances originated in the country including the most famous, the tango. Argentina lays claim to inventing the world-famous dance. Historically, the tango originated and took its first steps in the slaughterhouse district in Buenos Aires by the Rio de la Plata, the river that separates Argentina from Uruguay.

I was interested to discover that Argentina has in common with the rest of the world, Mother's Day and Father's Day but also Friend's Day. This is an occasion whereby all friends get together and have a party; this can carry on for some days in certain cases.

El Dia de Tradicion (The Day of Tradition) is a festival that is celebrated around November 10th each year, this festival celebrates the birth of Jose Hernandez, an Argentinean poet, who is considered to be one of the greatest literary figures of the country. The festival is a week-long and contains concerts, food, parades and parties. I pontificated that there is no Shakespeare's day, are we remiss in acknowledging his gift to us all with a day for the chance of a knees up? But then, where do we draw the line? How many other worthy contenders are there for a day off? Too costly to industry, though the treasury would do well out of booze sales, I'm sure. Returning my attention to the printed pages before me I must confess my ignorance here, I had no idea who Jose Hernandez was before reading this much less what he had written. I have never been really that interested in poetry, however, I took a moment to read his most famous poem Martin Fierro.

> I step not aside from the furrowed track,
> Though they loosen their hilts as they come;
> Let them speak me soft, I will answer soft,
> But the hard may find me a harder oft;
> In a fight they have found me as quick as they and quicker far than some.

I didn't doubt his skill but as this poem went on for 32 verses, I rather lost interest and so I skipped over this and went onto read about someone the whole world has heard of and who has helped to shape the modern day world and changed the lives of so many.

By now I had become totally transfixed by this New World Nation and managed one lunch time to pop into our local book shop. I found a book called "Politics of South and Central American Nations". It seemed an unlikely and surprising book to come across in rural England and was divided into sections by country. I snapped this up as it was the only book that covered Argentina that I could find and by now I had exhausted by own supply of material. Greedily like an addict after his next fix, I opened the book and savoured the smell of a new book. I flicked through the first few pages and started to read.

Ernesto "Che" Guevara. His face as we all know has been used and turned into an icon in popular culture for all kinds of revolutionary movements and ideologies. His image is printed on clothing, sprayed and painted on murals and hung on posters in bedrooms of angry and ideological students and youths around the world. The photograph most of these prints are based on was taken by Alberto Korda and named the most famous photograph in the world by Maryland Institute College of Art. Indeed his face is as famous as that of Fidel Castro, maybe more so, there are few around the world who would not be able to name his face. It's become such a popular image that some decades after his death, many people still walk around showing off his image on their clothing just in the name of fashion. He represents rebellion and individuality, his image becoming a romanticised vision of revolution. Some, myself included, would regard this as a blatant insult to his memory and all that he fought for, as I am sure that the majority of these "revolutionaries" haven't the first idea what his beliefs were and what he fought for, instead they just doggedly follow a protracted fashion ideal.

Guevara was a revolutionary for Marxism and is widely recognised as a central player in the Cuban Revolution. After medical school, he travelled throughout Latin America and the widespread and extreme poverty and inequalities amongst the people he saw inspired him to become a scholar of Marxism. This led him to Cuba where he and Castro were involved in revolutionary activities. Guevara died in Bolivia, executed by the Bolivian military in October 1967. Today, the Bolivians claim him as their own, as South America's poorest country, the underclasses love this man as one who tried to right their socioeconomic injustices.

Although his legacy is tied to his part in the Cuban Revolution, Guevara was not from Cuba, although they also love him as their own for the same reasons as the Bolivians. He was born south of Buenos Aires on 14 June 1928 and this is where he grew up and was educated. He was just 39 when he died, however, it struck me that he lived many lifetimes in such a short time and reading through some of his quotes. I was struck by the wisdom he had for one so young. I was particularly struck by:

To accomplish much you must first lose everything.

Live your life not celebrating victories but overcoming defeats.

Every day people straighten up the hair, why not the heart? And so the quotes continued.

Reading this made me think of my own fellow country man, Michael Collins, born in 1890 and sadly departed this earth at the tender age of 31 years. Not even a life time. Born in County Cork like me, he was also the youngest child like me. He was brought up a republican and was an Irish revolutionary soldier and later on a politician. He was very much the figure head for the Irish struggle for independence. Sadly, his beliefs like so many revolutionaries before him got him assassinated.

What is that saying? Only the good die young.

Say that today and people would look at you in horror as Michael Collins was part of Sinn Fein and was imprisoned for his beliefs and actions. He held some noticeable posts such as The Director of Intelligence of the Irish Republican Army. He was present in January 1919 when independence was declared of the Irish Republic. The ensuing war of independence is when his real fame came due to his skill in guerrilla warfare planning, directing and strategy. Depending on which side of the conflict you were on, he was hailed as a hero or terrorist. He was shot and killed in 1922 by anti-treaty forces while holding the position of commander-in chief of the National Army.

Bates, Bell, Buss, Cooper, Dexter, Lang, Lenham, Oakman, Parks, Shaw, Suttle and Thomson

12 April – 12st 1 – BP 123/60 – RHR 58 b/min

May 1995

My week followed its usual rhythm and while I still managed my daily coffees, Lorena was busy in the café. She always greeted me with tremendous enthusiasm and that made me feel rather special. Even though more often than not, she was rushed off her feet. She'd always find a moment for a quick chat, even though it was usually to ask me how I was and was it usual in this country for there to be so much rain. One day she joked that I should become a rice farmer, I'd be much richer. She walked away laughing. When she returned with my coffee, she asked, 'Why do you have so many names of such a small Island? You have Great Britain, The United Kingdom, what is all this about?' I felt at a bit of a loss to adequately answer this as it was not a point I had pondered before, so deflecting the question and deliberately leaving it unanswered. I told her the story of Albion and Brutus. She sat down delighted and enthralled by my story which I had to dig out for the recesses of my memory and as I recited it back to her, I could hear in my own mind, my mother telling me the same story at bedtime when I was a small boy as she tucked me up in preparation to going to sleep.

'Once upon a time, a young boy called Neptune loved the sea. Every chance he had, he played in the water, swimming and diving, jumping in the waves. When he grew up, he grew into a giant. He continued loving the sea and the sea and the waves in turn loved him. They made him their king.

'Neptune married a very beautiful woman called Amphitrite and together they had many sons. To each son when they were old enough to reign, he gave them an island in the sea.

'Now parents love all of their sons the same but there was one special son, who they both loved very much. His name was Albion and he was their fourth son. When he grew up, they wanted him to have a special island. They searched all of the seas, swimming far and wide to find the best island that there was.

'Hearing of their search, a young and a very beautiful mermaid searched for them and upon finding them, told them about the island she was from. She told them of its beauty, a small green island with white cliffs and yellow sands. This island was perfect and they instantly decided that this should be Albion's island and named it after him.

'Albion happily reigned for some years but then he was killed in a battle with Hercules. His parents, Neptune and Amphitrite, were heartbroken to lose their beloved son and cared for his island for many years after. Unfortunately, one day another giant, who was a bit of a thug, from Troy called Brutus came upon the island of Albion and declared it his own along with all small islands around it. He changed the name and declared it the Kingdom of Britain after his own name Brutus.

'Neptune lived for many years and never lost his love for Albion. When he was too old to rule anymore, he gave his sceptre to the islands of Britannia and that is where the song "Britannia rules the waves" comes from.'

Lorena laughed with childish delight at my fairy story and clapped her hands. 'Oh, what a lovely fable, I will never forget that. Do you think it answers my question?'

Bates, Bell, Buss, Cooper, Dexter, Lang, Lenham, Oakman, Parks, Shaw, Suttle and Thomson

15 April – 12st – BP 117/60 – RHR 78 b/min
May 1995

I confided in her, one Saturday, that I felt very frustrated by how little care people took of their health. Surely health was a gift to be treasured and not taken for granted. Increasingly my patients were complaining of afflictions to do with a sedentary lifestyle coupled with too much sugar and fat. I despaired at the stupidity of some of my patients but there were others who would not want to bother me but who should have brought their conditions to my attention sooner when more could have been done.

When I had told her this, she had laughed at me and told me that I had clearly not taken my exams in being God but once I had them, all would be well. I was mildly offended at being laughed at but I tried to hide my irritation with a smile. I wasn't often mocked and it was a new experience that I didn't really care for.

Sensing my slightly sour mood, she pulled up a chair with a flourish, sat down and leaned forwards with her elbows on her knees and her chin cradled in her hands. 'Let me tell you about Tango!' The abrupt change to the conversation took me slightly off guard and the truth was, at that moment, I really didn't want to hear about Tango. I had read a bit and knew as much as I ever wanted to about this topic. However, I was left with no option as she whisked me away to the dance halls of Buenos Aires, dropping her voice so that it sounded very husky and sensual.

'The Tango is described as a sultry and intimate dance for two people. Its moves and music are seductive and passionate and you can recognise it by the close embrace between dance partners; its movements are quick and precise. At first, the upper classes ignored this dance and thought of it as a dance of the poor people. But we know better, no Doctor? The poor people knew how to dance and the influence of Tango grew from the ghettos of Buenos Aires the dance became so popular. It spread to the poor communities of the working people of the city and from there it was in all the dance halls.

'It was the first couple dance that called for, what is the word when you invent a bit as you go along? You guess a bit the next movements in time to the music? I know an improvisation. It was the first dance for a couple where you could express freely and use improvisation.

'In 1912, Paris fell in amour with our dance, the French were jealous of our dance, they "stole" it and tried to make it their own and they made it famous. The French they tried to steal it but it is ours and Tango is now the most famous dance in the world, well maybe.' Lorena winked at me at this bit and laughed, signalling a possible exaggeration of facts. 'And it started out in the brothels of Buenos Aires!'

Jumping to her feet, she looked round and shouted, 'Donatella, come here, quickly!' In alarm, thinking possibly that the café was on fire or there was a complaint, Donatella rushed forward with surprising agility for one so large.

'Doctor, what is wrong?' she queried almost on the point of tears. Before I could shed any light on the matter, Lorena grabbed Donatella's left hand with her right hand and somehow placed Donatella's right hand around her slim middle while she herself reached around and placed her left hand in the small of Donatella's back.

'Donatella, dance tango with me!' Lorena commanded.

'Stupid girl, what are you doing? I have a café to run. We don't have time for nonsense.'

Lorena not easily put off, surged forwards in the direction of where her right hand pointed with a poised and domineering posture, sweeping Donatella along with her. After the initial power struggle that ensured, Donatella giggled and allowed herself to be embraced and joined in this dance. I reflected that they made an odd looking couple, a tall, slim and attractive girl with a short and plump matronly looking woman of advancing years. One with long flowing dark hair and the other with a pert bun stuck on the top of her head.

As they ricocheted around the café, drawing applause from the other patrons, I couldn't help but be taken by the sense of seriousness and emotion that they both displayed. They both stared intently into each other's eyes, never loosing that contact. Suddenly, they both came to a grinding halt and dropping their arms, both erupted into raucous and heart felt laughter. The café got to its feet laughing and applauding with cries of "More".

Slightly breathless and flushed from her antics, Lorena approached me with a twinkle in her eyes, reaching her arms out to me she coyly and saucily invited me with a "Doctor" in that same husky and slightly sensual tone of voice. In spite of myself, I laughed nervously, slightly embarrassed and getting up from my chair, politely declined her offer and disappeared off to see more patients.

That evening, I managed to find some more information on the Tango and while Lorena's account had strictly speaking been accurate. I found some further insights into it. Before this dance craze spread through Europe in the early twentieth-century, it almost certainly had been a dance reserved for prostitutes who strutted their stuff with clients. This theory of the history of the tango, one argument stated that it doesn't take into account the other places where working-class men and women went to dance in the working-class neighbourhoods of Buenos Aires, suggesting that although it was a dance used in brothels, the common people were also enjoying its moves. Regardless, what is known is that the tango is a dance whose early days were all about sex and gender relations. The women and men, who danced, were playing out social roles through their "improvised" movements.

Breathless – Bates, Bell, Buss, Cooper, Dexter, Lang, Lenham, McCarthy, Oakman, Parks, Shaw and Suttle

18 April – 12st – BP 120/60

The next evening returning to my newly acquired book along with my bottle of Santa Ana red, a Malbec wine from the Mendoza region, I found out that in 1816, the United Provinces of the Rio Plata declared their independence from Spain. After Bolivia, Paraguay and Uruguay went their separate ways, the area that remained became Argentina. The country's population and culture were heavily shaped by immigrants from throughout Europe but most particularly Italy and Spain, which provided the largest percentage of newcomers from 1860 to 1930. Apparently, the Spanish spoken in Argentina, though grammatically the same as other Spanish speaking countries, is spoken with much more emphasis and flare than in the neighbouring counties.

Argentina is governed under a federal presidential constitutional republic. Argentina wrote its own Declaration of Independence and established its own government after declaring independence from Spain in July 1816. Then, in 1856, they established a constitution that is still used today in the country. *José de San Martín* or The Protector of the South is considered to be the most famous person of Argentina. He is known for leading South America to freedom from Spanish rule. I pondered this and thought that this was probably true to Argentinians but highly unlikely that anyone outside of the country would even know this fact. I consider myself a well-read man but I had never heard of this man before now.

Today, the government is comprised of a president, vice president and supreme court president. Argentina also has a legislature that contains congress, senate and a chamber of deputies. Up until about the mid-twentieth-century, much of Argentina's history was dominated by periods of internal political conflict between Federalists and Unitarians and between civilian and military factions.

Juan Perón was the president at the time of the Second World War and went on to have a subsequent two terms in office; these were some years apart.

My only knowledge to this point about Perón was that he had a wife called Evita and she was made famous by a musical by Andrew Lloyd Webber, a woman who fought for the under classes.

Yawning deeply, I regretfully laid down my book, face down and undoubtedly creasing the spine. I had never understood the obsession by people who insisted on keeping books and looking as if they had never been read. I was stunned to note that the wine bottle was empty. I enjoyed a drink but it was usually just a couple of glasses. Oh, well, a lovely bottle to accompany another interesting insight into this far away and foreign land. In a contented state of mind I looked at my trophy and felt that familiar tingle of pleasure go down my spine. I got up and walked over to the mantel piece and picked it up. I allowed my fingers to run over the engraving and although the letters were too small to trace out each individual letter, I could feel McCarthy spelt out under my thumb. I put it back down and turned around, switched off the lights and went to bed.

23 12st Cramp – Terrible Nightmares Exhausted

I feel ill and dizzy writing this, like I am in a tunnel; the walls are closing in and there is a fog in front of my eyes.

Dexter, Langridge, Lenham, Oakman and Thomson.
One Sunday in May 1995

I awoke feeling refreshed and inspired, though looking outside it was a dismal day. It was Sunday and I contemplated my options. Usually on a Sunday I tried to go for a brisk ten mile walk and then reward myself with a pint at The Rose and Crown. I knew that Donatello's was closed today and wondered what Lorena did on her days off. I didn't fancy the great outdoors today, so put on a news program and read my way through the papers. The hours passed and once I had found a pork pie hiding in the fridge for lunch, I brewed myself a pot of tea and resumed my reading about the politics of Argentina.

Bates, Bell, Buss, Cooper, Dexter, Langridge, Lenham, Oakman, Parks, Shaw, Suttle and Thomson

27 April 2016 – 12st 2 – BP 120/63 – RHR 59 b/min

After World War II, an era of Peronist authoritarian rule and ongoing meddling in subsequent governments was followed by a military junta that took power in 1976. After the death of Juan Perón in 1974, he was succeeded by his third wife, Isabel Perón. In March 1976, five days after Isabel was deposed, a military junta took over the presidency, closing the national congress, imposing censorship and trade unions were banned bringing the state and municipal government under military control. Meanwhile, General Videla, who now filled the top spot, initiated a campaign against any suspected dissidents. When the military took control, so began a period known as The Dirty War, an infamous campaign waged from 1976 to 1983 by Argentina's military dictatorship against suspected left-wing political opponents, both real and imagined.

It has been estimated that between 10,000 and 30,000 citizens were killed, many of them "disappeared without trace" seized by the authorities and today the search for these souls tirelessly continues by their heartbroken loved ones. The targets were students, militants, trade unionists, writers, journalists, artists, Marxists and left-wing activists. Throughout the country the regime set up hundreds of detention camps, where thousands of people were jailed and persecuted. Leftist guerrillas had been widely active in the country in the late 1960s, therefore, the Argentine government claimed that it was fighting a legitimate civil war. Initially there was little opposition but this began to change in the late 1970s, as the evidence of civil rights violations began to grow.

During his years as US Secretary of State, Henry Kissinger had congratulated Argentina's military junta for combating The Left, stating that in his opinion, 'The government of Argentina had done an outstanding job in wiping out terrorist forces.'

A particularly vocal critic of both left and right-wing violence was Adolfo Pérez Esquivel, who was arrested and tortured in 1977 and later went on to receive the Nobel Peace Prize in 1980. For the most part, however, opposition was choked off by the blanket rigorous censorship, strict curfews and an overwhelming fear of the secret police. I mused for a moment and considered how many other countries today suffered the same problems. Egypt, Iraq, Russia, China, Burma, the list goes on and is certainly not exclusive. Sadly, this is not an uncommon story, yet is totally alien to countries where freedom of speech is given. If ever we are all to be motivated to fight for something and be jealous to protect a right, then surely this has to be the most worthy of all.

Videla was succeeded in 1981 by Viola, who, with the Dirty War nearing its end, was unable to control his military allies. In December he was shouldered aside by Galtieri who was presented with a slumping economy and increasing civil opposition to military rule. In a bid to deflect attention, he launched Argentina's disastrous invasion of the Falkland (Malvinas) Islands and he was then removed from office three days after the conflict ended in June 1982. I remember a university lecturer who had clearly gone off the point broadly claiming that 'A good war is what any failing economy needs. It ignites a sense of nationalism and people forget their own woes for the greater good of the country. However, it is imperative to win or you will be worse off than you were before.' Bignone was installed as president not long after. Under Bignone, political parties were permitted to resume their activities and general elections were announced, meanwhile, sectors of the armed forces worked around the clock to conceal any evidence of crimes committed by their own during the Dirty War.

Democracy returned to Argentina when Alfonsín of a major centre left political party, won the presidential election of 1983. Not long after his inauguration, he reversed legislation passed by Bignone, announcing plans to prosecute members from the former military governments, including former presidents, Videla, Viola and Galtieri, all of whom were extremely right wing military men. He repealed a law granting amnesty to those accused of crimes and human rights violations during the Dirty War, hundreds of military personnel were prosecuted. In the trial of nine former junta members in 1985, five were convicted including Videla and Viola. Galtieri was acquitted in that trial but in 1986 he was convicted along with two other officers for incompetency in the Falkland Islands War.

I stopped for a moment here to ponder the meaning and implications of democracy. A word that we throw about with careless abandon in modern day Europe with no real thought for its implications.

I looked it up in my Oxford English Dictionary and it stated:

'A system of government by the whole population or all the eligible members of a state, typically through elected representatives.

- A state governed under a system of democracy.
- Control of an organisation or group by the majority of its members.
- The practice or principles of social equality.'

I considered this and the following points occurred to me.

Theoretically, all people are created equal; their environments and circumstances cannot be, so their thoughts based on their surroundings and upbringing will be different. We assume all opinions are equal and carry the same weight and consideration. Thus the assumption must be drawn that everyone can arrive at what are perceived rational and informed decisions. Can we all whole-heartedly accept this to be true? Clearly not if for no other reason than the facts stated in the first sentence here.

A problem with democracy is that in the end, it inevitably becomes a popularity contest by political candidates. Polls don't decide who the best is for all, more often it is won by whoever is most willing to say what people like to hear more often than not bribing the populace with improbable and empty promises. Sadly but inevitably, many candidates to political office play to the popular vote, highlighting policies that revolve around the immediate satisfaction of the masses instead of long-term more crucial improvements.

Hunting around my books, I came across one on philosophy which stated that according to economist Kenneth Arrow, pure democracy cannot work. He demonstrated the theorem in his doctoral thesis and popularised it in his 1951 book "Social Choice and Individual Values". The original paper was titled "A Difficulty in the Concept of Social Welfare". According to this theorem, so long as there are more than two candidates, there is no possible voting system that can ensure the satisfaction of three crucial criteria for fairness:

-   If every voter prefers alternative X over alternative Y, then the group prefers X over Y.
-   If every voter's preference between X and Y remains unchanged, then the group's preference between X and Y will also remain unchanged.
-   There is no "dictator", no single voter possesses the power to always determine the group's preference.

If these criteria are left unsatisfied, it effectively means that democracy—at least in its purest form—cannot work.

Gazing at my trophy I concluded that in simple terms, there will always be a winner and a loser and will the loser and possibly others who get lost in between always accept the result and will the winner always be the true majority.

Sir Thomas More beheaded at The Tower of London by Henry VIII in 1535, had been the chancellor and a much trusted and loved friend of this flamboyant King. However, as a devoted and learned man of great principle, he could not accept the separation of England from the Church in Rome. The divorce of Henry from his first of six wives, Catherine of Aragon and his proposed marriage to Anne Boleyn, a protestant, was a step too far for him. Henry pleaded with his friend to just accept what Henry wanted and at least at face value go along with him. Finally, Henry felt that to have such a powerful and influential man opposed to his actions posed too greater risk to his success and effectively removed him from the situation. As a scholar, More wrote several books; one of which and possibly his most famous, Utopia. He set out his vision of a fair and equal society. Unfortunately, his vision for a democratic state was rather more communist and as we increasingly see, communist states are just as prone to abuse and repression of the majority, so it gets no closer to the Greek ideal of Power to the People.

Bates, Bell, Buss, Langridge, Lenham, Suttle and Thomson

April 30 – 11st 13– BP
132/71 – Confused

Returning my attention to the book in my lap, I read on that under increased pressure from the military. President Alfonsín pushed two amnesty laws through the national congress passed in the mid-80s. The first set a deadline for introducing new prosecutions, while the second granted immunity to hundreds of military officers below the rank of colonel, who were determined to have been following orders. (Exceptions were made for cases of rape or the abduction of babies). However, rebellion broke out within the military in 1987, followed by more revolts in 1988 as the military were pushed to extremes over wages, inadequate equipment and the trials of fellow members dating back to the Dirty War.

Alfonsín resigned in 1989 and was succeeded by Menem the same year. He immediately pardoned Videla and other top officers convicted of abuses during the Dirty War. The recent political history resembled a game of snakes and ladders or so it seemed. In later years, long after this story ended, I went on to read that Videla later was charged with kidnapping babies and giving them to childless military couples during his regime. He was placed under house arrest in the late 1990s and sent to prison some 10 years later after a judge revoked his house arrest status. Viola and Galtieri died before Argentina's supreme court voted to repeal the amnesty laws passed by Alfonsín. Hundreds of military officers were tried and several convicted. In 2007, Bignone was charged with human rights abuses and taken into custody, convicted in 2010 and given a 25 year sentence. A couple of years later, Videla, Bignone and others were found guilty of the systematic abduction of babies born to political prisoners. Videla was given a 50 year sentence, Bignone 50 years.

Democracy so called started to return in 1983 and has since held fast despite numerous challenges. In the nineties, sixty percent of adults were classified as being below the poverty line as a result of rampant inflation which is a problem that has endured for many years and still to this day is a blight to this troubled economy.

An economist is quoted as saying, 'Argentina will always have financial troubles while all the power and wealth is held by a few who exploit it to their own gain. More importantly until Argentina realises its own potential strength on the world stage given the tremendous natural resources that it has at its fingertips, it will continuously blunder from one grasping leader to another. Argentina needs to start believing in her own strength and ability, only then will she succeed.'

Yawning I looked at the clock, surprised how the time had passed. I had read my way past midnight and the tea pot was now cold and undrinkable. I felt stiff and my back ached. I regretted the missed opportunity of my weekly walk earlier but felt stimulated by all that I had read. My mind was buzzing with my newly acquired knowledge and the new academic quandaries that had arisen in my mind about a land that until some weeks ago, I had paid no attention to.

Bates, Bell, Buss, Dexter, Langridge, Lenham, Oakman, Parks, Shaw, Suttle and Thomson

May 3 – 11st 13– BP 132/71 – RHR 78 b/min
May 1995

Presenting myself as usual, the next week after our last chat, Lorena was again able to take me away with her words to her world, so very far away from my own. She enthusiastically told me all about her family, their family estancia where they raise beef and grow grapes. Her childhood which sounded idyllic with fun and action packed adventures with her brother and sister. She told me about her older sister, Florencia, who is a journalist with a particular interest in politics and history and her younger brother, Gustavo, a talented sportsman with a love of football and motorbikes was in a sport academy with the hopes of achieving sporting greatness. She spoke of them with huge pride and deep affection. That familiar stab of jealousy stabbed me in the gut. I shook it off and focused on her loved and cherished family memory.

'In the summer we all go by horse back into the hills and mountains, where there is a beautiful lake, it is surrounded by pine trees and we dig a big hole, fill it with fire wood and then with a big metal cross roast a sheep over it. In Argentina, this is called an Asado, you call it a barbecue. It takes many hours to cook and while we wait, we take the horses swimming in the lake. At the far end of the lake, some years we see flamingos with their beautiful pink feathers. There are different breeds of this bird and they are amazing, really fantastic you know? In the trees there are many birds and the smell of the pine resin in the heat is very lovely.' She had a distant and wistful look as she told me this and I wondered if she was maybe a little homesick.

Her parents were the children of immigrants and born in Argentina. Her father's family had settled in the western part of the country and grew wine and raised cattle. Her mother's family had moved to the capital. It seems that her parents had met and fallen in love while both attending the University of Mendoza, a name with which I was now very familiar as I was increasingly on first name terms with a few of the wines of the region. The politics of their country seemed to have passed this family by and I very much got the impression that they were a rather wealthy family.

From her descriptions of the family estancia, it seemed like there was a long private track which led up to the periphery. There were high gates which were usually always open and from here on there was a long drive way which was shrouded on either side by 50 ft. high eucalyptus trees. On the hot days, the smell was intoxicating and it was always cool under the trees. Here the three children would ride their bikes, run races, bounce along on their skate boards and generally play the games that children do. Later on, her brother Gustavo would challenge his sisters to races on motorbikes.

Their mother looked after the cattle side of the family business and their father ran the vineyards. They had a successful red called Mabel Ines which is named after the vineyard. It seemed as if the children were actively involved in both businesses, rounding up cattle, Gustavo on his motorbike and his sisters on horseback. During grape picking season, everyone was expected to drop what other commitments they had and put in long hours bringing in that year's harvest.

I was reminded about a story, a patient of mine had told me some years ago. He had recently returned from spending some time in Australia, travelling about and working, picking fruit and vegetables and in the right season, grapes. He found himself in Southern Australia and picked grapes for a family run vineyard. He was short of cash and they didn't really need him but taking pity on the young English man, they employed him for a couple of weeks. He told me about the lovely friendly atmosphere working with the Semmler family and their pickers. Apparently, the vineyard had been in the family for a couple of generations and produced the Dutschks wines but under the currently leadership of Ken Semmler, they had gone on to produce a wine called Willowbend and this was now considered to be one of the premier wines of the Barossa Valley. Interestingly, the Barossa Valley is called after the Barrosa Ridge in Andalusia in Spain. I was always on the lookout for this wine and I had managed to get hold of a bottle of white once. I didn't usually drink white but one hot day, I partook in a couple of glasses and thoroughly enjoyed it.

My young patient had been so delighted to be a part of their team and so inspired by their kindness. He told me that they are Lutherans. This surprised me as my thoughts about

Lutherans were based on my scant knowledge of Martin Luther, who opposed the Catholic Church and as a slack member of the Catholic Church, I had been brought up to believe that everyone who opposed the Catholic Church were fundamentally bad people and not to be trusted. I took the time to find out about Lutherans a bit more and couldn't help but think that by the end of my research that Herr Luther may have had a very good point or two. To my mind he had been a revolutionary and a radical, which seemed to be traits at odds with the kind and gentle nature of the Australian grape growing family that my young patient told me about.

My brief research into the matter informed me that, Martin Luther was a German professor of Theology, a monk, a priest and a prominent figure in the protestant reformation. He rejected many of the teachings of the Roman Catholic Church and strongly objected to their views on indulgences. I knew all about indulgences from my slog through my catholic upbringing. These indulgences are the remission of a temporal punishment brought about by sin punishment and consists of either earthly sufferings or time spent after death in Purgatory, a fate considered worse than death itself. These are issued by the church and given to an individual who has demonstrated some type of penance or good work. Indulgences can be applied to oneself or to the soul of a deceased person.

He wrote widely on the matter and was excommunicated from the church. His teachings were that salvation could only be earned not by good deeds but only by God's grace through the believer's faith in Jesus Christ. Those, who follow his wider teachings and beliefs, are called Lutherans. He went on to marry a former nun. He died in 1546 aged over 50 years old.

I had drifted off into my own world and shook myself, metaphorically speaking, and started to concentrate again on what Lorena was saying to me. Apparently, her mother had a passion for beautifully scented roses and had created a rose garden between the end of the eucalyptus drive way and the front door of the Estancia. Clearly, she was quite dedicated to her passion and had bred different roses, each of which she called after her three children.

'Florencia's rose is yellow, bright yellow, so yellow if you stare at it too long it hurts your eyes. My rose is a very dark red, almost purple or black. It has many petals and they are very compact. Gustavo's is good too; his is orange. It is very big and a little floppy, the inside when it is older goes white. His smells nice but I love mine the best.

'Mute always says that there is nothing wrong with beauty and perfection is in the eyes of the beholder but what makes real perfection are the flaws that the beauty overcomes.

'In each of our roses, she bred in a flaw. Florencia's are the vicious thorns, mine only lasts for a couple of days and Gustavo's fade fast and lose their colour. They go from orange to white.' I struggled to understand why anyone would deliberately breed in such obvious faults, especially when she clearly had the know how to ensure that these flowers would be so much better without these deliberate slip ups. I wanted to ask about this but Lorena was several topics on now and was describing home life.

No matter what, at 1 pm every day, the whole family sat down to lunch together. It sounded like a complicated affair as her grandmother on her father's side only spoke Italian but by all accounts could understand any under hand comments made in Spanish. It sounded like a rather traditional Latin family set up. They would finish their meal by drinking *Herba de Maté*. To you and I, tea, only the manner in which they drink this appalled me.

'You put the Maté leaves in the bottom of the cup. It is a special cup, usually wood, but it can be metal but this gets too hot to hold. You put in the hot water and if you want to, sugar, you then drink this through a special metal straw called a Bombilla. You then give it to the person next to you and they fill it up and drink through the Bombilla.'

'The same straw?'

'Well, yes, of course.' Thank goodness this was not likely to catch on this country controlling the spread of colds is hard enough without everyone sharing drinking straws!

'You know drinking Maté is a fundamental part of Argentinean culture. It is very much a part of who we are. To share Maté with someone is a sign that you accept them. You are both at ease with one another. You share your stories and opinions and thoughts and your hopes and dreams with each other.' Lorena was speaking so earnestly, trying so hard to make me understand this important trait in her fellow countrymen's culture, which frankly was utterly lost on me and seems all unnecessarily pointless.

'Maté teas are very good for you too. Maté has health qualities. It is an appetite suppressant and you can get your own Maté mixed up with different herbs and flowers to suit your taste and health needs. It's also very good to help with altitude sickness.' This all sounds a bit too far-fetched to me rather like some Chinese teas which claim impossible and improbable outcomes. Still I kept my thoughts to myself.

Lorena went on to explain the running of the Estancia and told me how she would cry and be upset when the grounds men would set traps and put down poison to keep the local wild life away from the cattle. Puma attacks were not uncommon and with carcasses brought Condors and other scavengers, which in turn resulted in the death of these creatures through eating the poison. This upset her greatly. Apparently, guanacos, a type of camelid roam wild throughout the country and often get caught in the miles barbed wire fences that crisscross the land, resulting in a slow and agonising death.

I asked if she had any family photos so that I could get a mental picture of all the people she was telling me about. She promised to bring in the photos that she stored under her mattress with her passport for safe keeping, so she would always know where they were!

Realising my strengthening interest in her life and foreign world, most days young Lorena would bound up to me and impart a fleeting anecdote or two before rushing off to serve another customer but in these brief moments, she built a picture of her family and life in Mendoza. She said it was good for her to practice her English and I think she enjoyed talking about her family. She clearly loved them all deeply and it was evident that she missed them all. Barely pausing for breath, she flipped from subject to subject and not missing a beat. Her evident delight about the subject in hand caused her to light up and her enthusiastic manner brought each person to life.

Like any family, they holidayed together. These family holidays seemed to revolve predominantly around a place called Bariloche, some hours south of Mendoza. In winter, which was during our summer, they would go skiing here and in the summer, our winter, they would enjoy weeks of hiking in the hills there in many national parks. Apparently, the lake around which Bariloche is situated is at its most beautiful in springtime when the snow-capped mountains surrounding it frame the backdrop to the deep blue water, which in turn is off set by the vivid yellow and purple wild lupines, which stretch for miles and the golden-coloured broom which grows everywhere. Unexpectedly, Lorena carried on,

'Many Germans went to live in Bariloche after the world war, the second one, and now as a result, we have the best chocolate in the world there now. Honestly, there is no better chocolate anywhere, I promise you this!' She said this with such defiance. I didn't dare try to contradict her. She rattled on to the next or the never ending stream of facts.

'In Bariloche, they also produce a lot of rose hips. It is made into many things, including face cream. This is why all Argentinean women have such wonderful skin.' This was said in such a matter of fact way and so unconsciously. I peered at her skin, which was smooth and unblemished and glowed with health in a way that only the youthful can, so I concluded that it must be true. Whether or not, the rose hip cream had anything to do with it, who knew, maybe it was just good genes from Latin stock.

I reflected on her relationship with her siblings and compared it to my own relationship with Denis. Listening to Lorena proudly tell me about Florencia and Gustavo, I realised suddenly that I had always been jealous of Denis. It was an unpleasant realisation and I pondered at the source of this jealousy. His good looks, charismatic personality and professional and sporting success had given others someone to compare me to, so when my accident happened, I was pitied all the more. A fact, that now I realise, had made me bitter and angry, his successful marriage contrasted painfully with my own as well.

I pondered the past and it occurred to me that maybe we could have been closer, had I not been so jealous and thinking back. I realised that he had treated me with nothing other than kindness and affection. It saddened me to discover that I could have probably have had a far closer relationship with him. His wife always wrote to me at Christmas and birthdays with family photos and stories of their life and the upbringing of their daughter, whose name I never remember. With some regret, I now wish I had read those letters and not thrown away the photos. In fact, I'm not sure when I last heard from them or even where they now live.

Bates, Bell, Buss, Dexter, Langridge, Lenham, Oakman, Parks, Shaw and Thomson

May 30 – 11st 7– BP 135/89 – RHR 79 b/min
May 1995

The next day after the promise of photos, I eagerly arrived for my coffee. I would have to be quick as I had a full diary as usual but even more so, as Sarah had squeezed in a couple of extra visits due to an outbreak of something that seemed rather unpleasant and had all the signs of being highly contagious. Along with my coffee, Lorena gave me a budging envelope of photos. 'I cannot show you them myself; we are too busy today.' She gestured around the room which was cheek by jowl. Sardonically, as I looked around the heaving café, I wondered how many people were about to go down with the projectile symptoms by all congregating in the same place, most of whom had undoubtedly poor hygiene habits.

'I wrote all the names of my family on the backs of the pictures, you can take them home and look at them later, give them back to me when you next come for coffee.' With that, she dashed off to serve a particularly demanding group who had already had more than enough cake and coffee looking at the state of the table. Excited to see the photos later, I carefully placed the envelope in my Gladstone bag and finishing the last of my coffee, left the café to see to my patients.

All day I had to bite down the feeling of excitement, a feeling I remember as a child on Christmas Eve, knowing that the next day there would be presents for me to open. The best part of Christmas was the anticipation of what was to come. Most situations where we look forwards to something are often more enjoyable than the actual event. I was later than usual that evening, it had been a tiring and quite taxing day, a wonderful old boy in the village was displaying some symptoms which concerned me greatly and I knew in my heart, that once the results were back, I would have a very painful conversation breaking the heart wrenching news to him and his equally delightful but very frail wife of 62 years.

I opened the fridge and couldn't face the chicken and ham pie that awaited me there, so I poured myself a glass of Mendoza red from the vineyard of Maria Alicia from the Las Compuertas region. The label on the bottle informed me that I would detect hints of pepper and peach and that the wine was best enjoyed with red meat and strong cheese. Pepper and peach! What a hideous combination and I had no red meat or cheese, so an empty stomach would just have to do and taking the photos from my bag put on my reading glasses and settled myself in my chair. I had already tried several different Argentinian wines, replacing my usual French Cotes de Rhone and Cahors with these new world delights. Taking a sip, I concluded that it was a very pleasant wine, though strong and with a strong after taste but one I was sure to partake of on many more occasions.

Taking the photos out, I could see that they were very dog-eared and bent around the edges. Clearly they had been shown many times and the gloss on the surface had all been worn away. They were not all very clear and some of the photos were evidently quite elderly. They showed typical family scenes, everyone smiling and looking at the photographer. Robust was a word that sprang to mind looking at the photos, everyone looked very robust, tanned, healthy and remarkably happy. They were a good looking crew and I was intrigued to notice that Lorena's mother was petit and blonde. Everyone else in the family was dark but she appeared delicate and golden by comparison. One thing that I did notice about the lovely fragile looking lady was that it seemed as if she had different coloured eyes; they were pale so unlike the dark brown eyes of her family. I wasn't sure as the photo was not clear but it looked as if one eye was grey or pale blue and the other was a hazel or green.

As I said, the photos were not great quality and much loved and well looked at, so years of thumb prints had knocked off the sheen and clarity, which might have been once there. As I worked my way through the photos, I came across some black and white photos. These were even harder to decipher but as I moved from one photo to the next, I took in a sharp breath. The photo of the man before me made me shudder. He was from what I could tell fair, with icy eyes. Everything about him was rigid and severe. His hair was very short and his suit starched. I couldn't put my finger on it, why I had such a dramatic reaction to his photo and turning it over to read who it was. I noted that this was Lorena's grandfather, Frederick Rubio, her mother's father. Hence the blonde hair and pale eyes. I checked back through the photos to the one of Lorena's mother and her apparently different coloured eyes but it was impossible to tell from the black and white photo if this was a characteristic that she shared with her father. It struck me that they didn't look at all like the other members of the family, who clearly were from Southern European stock, I wondered at his origins. His looks suggested possibly a German or Northern European ancestry.

It was only as I reached for my glass and realised it was empty, an increasingly common theme that was accompanying my new area of interest. With that I looked at my watch and discovered that I had been absorbed in this family's photos for the better part of two hours. I considered my options and reflected that it was as good a time as any to have a hot shower and go to bed. Carefully picking up the photos and putting them back into the envelope, I placed this much treasured package back into my bag and pottered off to the bathroom and on to bed. I rarely dream and generally sleep soundly but that night was marred by constant tossing and turning, I couldn't get comfortable and when I drifted off, Grandfather, Rubio, was glaring at me in his piercing way.

The reaction I had to his image reminded me of my aunt, who had told me I was a spoilt brat. I had hated her as a child; she would pinch my cheeks hard and yank on my ears in a non-affectionate way. She would always try to catch me out and belittle me. I was scared of her when I was little and she knew it. She never missed an opportunity to try and make me cry. I was shattered when I got up in the morning.

Bates, Bell, Buss, Dexter, Lang, Lenham, Oakman, Parks, Shaw, Suttle and Thomson

2 June – 11st 7– BP 135/90
– RHR 80 b/min
Towards the end of May 1995

By the time I got to Donatella's, I was running very late. I felt crumpled and a bit out of sorts. It was heaving in there and coupled with the fact that I didn't have the time today to enjoy my coffee. I left the photos with Lorena and said that I would be back tomorrow when it was a bit quieter and we would be able to talk more. She gave me her brilliant smile and stowed away the budging envelope of photos into the front of her apron. The rest of my day was a blur as I hurried from appointment to appointment and never seemed to catch up. Unusually for me, I went straight to bed that night, exhausted beyond normal expectations.

Over the next couple of weeks of coffees and one Saturday lunch time, Lorena continued to tell me more about her family and country. I could tell that she loved to talk about her homeland and loved ones and spoke with so much pride. I had taken to correcting her English from time to time, as her word order was quite muddled, especially the more excited and emotional she got. She took it all with good grace.

Over lunch on Saturday, I took Lorena to the Rose and Crown and we sat in the beer garden and savoured the delights of their ploughman's lunch. I have always enjoyed a good ploughman's with mature cheddar. The Rose and Crown prided themselves on their ingredients and the cheddar was so strong that it could split and blister your tongue. I think Lorena was less enchanted with the meal as she said she found it a bit heavy and stodgy. However, she was delighted by the beer garden itself as it had a very English country garden air. She boldly ordered a half a pint of local cider which I am sure still had twigs and apple cores in it. Surely that was the heavy and stodgy aspect of the meal? She bravely swallowed it down. I couldn't help but notice as I sipped my beer that she had increasingly rosy cheeks.

After some chit chat I wanted to tackle the subject of Grandfather, Rubio, and asked where he was from originally as he looked so different from the rest of the family but instead I asked about her mother.

'Yes, you are right, the rest of the family, we are all so strong and we are all dark but my mother is very slim; my sister and I, we are always so annoyed that we cannot be more like her.'

I looked at Lorena with some surprise at this comment, for if she were any slimmer, I would think that she possibly had an eating disorder, so I concluded that she was referring to the bird like and fragile frame that her mother had rather than actual body weight.

'Is your mother like your grandfather then?' I prompted. She looked thoughtful.

'In looks maybe, though my mother is filled with love. She is like my Abuelita.' Again this struck me as a usual thing to say but thinking about those scary eyes of his, I thought I understood.

'Was your grandfather very harsh then?' Once I had explained the meaning of harsh, Lorena again looked thoughtful.

'I did not know my grandfather; he died in Paraguay before I was born. My grandparents lived in Buenos Aires which is two days away from us and often he went to Paraguay.'

'Oh, did he holiday there then?'

'My grandfather was a doctor and he was involved in some research. I don't know but he had a good friend who was also a research doctor and they would work together.'

'How very interesting, you don't know what kind of research?' She laughed at me.

'Do you know what your grandfather used to do?' Point taken, who knows or even cares as a youngster what their grandparents did. I concluded that Frederick Rubio and his friend probably did research into jungle borne illnesses as this seemed a reasonable explanation.

I wanted to ask more about this, as I thought that it would be of interest to know about their work but I could tell I had reached a dead end and Lorena was clearly disinterested in the line that the conversation had taken.

I only vaguely recall my own grandfather. In my mind's eye, he is shrouded in shadows but I do remember his hands, they were so soft. He always wore a tie and had a gold chain and fob watch. His monocle would stay in place for hours as if by magic and no matter how much I tried to practice with a drink top, I could only ever keep it in place for a few seconds at a time. I'd spend hours practicing scrunching up my face and contorting it into ridiculous expressions in the hope of keeping the bottle top in place, only for it to always fall out before I had even moved my hands away from my face.

'So, tell me about Granny, Rubio. Abuelita?'

'This is where my mother got her lovely spirit from; Abuelita was so kind. She loved us all so much that she would cry and cry when we left her. She made beautiful cakes for us and was always knitting us clothes. She didn't talk much, my mother said that she always did whatever my grandfather told her to do, you know and he may have been a bit of a bully to her.' Having seen his photo, I didn't doubt it. I remembered a dark dumpy lady from the photo who had a slightly gypsy look to her.

'Was Abuelita her name?' I queried, Lorena laughed.

'You know I don't know what her name was, Abuela is the Spanish for Grandmother and if you put ITA on the end. It makes the word loving and little, so in English it would mean Little Granny but more loving than that.' This was a linguistic complexity that was entirely new to me and I wasn't really that sure that I understood what she meant.

At this point, I asked about her mother's eyes.

'Yes, she has one blue and one green eye; we call her Mamma Mute. You know after the Malamute dogs, they have different coloured eyes and similar to huskies; they are strong and brave like wolves.' It was an affectionately told family anecdote and seemed to suit her mother's looks very well.

Lorena suddenly turned to me and laughed. 'I have talked too much, now it is your turn; tell me all about this insane game which I really don't understand at all, that goes on for days, tell me about cricket. I understand that you are very good, a bit of an expert.' She looked at me expectantly with a lovely big smile. Internally I felt the doors starting to slam shut like a prison lock down when the alarm has just sounded. I looked down at my hands as I did not wish to discuss one of the big loves of my life with this delightful girl. It was too personal and too private, it just hurt too much.

'My dear, if you don't mind I'll get the bill now unless you would like anything else?' Seemingly unaware of my inner turmoil, she happily walked with me to the bar and chattered the whole time while I paid the bill. She then suggested a walk back to the bowling green to watch the match that was in progress. She talked non-stop about the rules that she had found out from Frankie. I was intensely grateful for this as it gave me time to compose myself and control my internal disquiet about raking up my own past. She fell silent and we watched the men and women before us in their bowling whites for some time.

Without any prompting at all, Lorena began to tell me about visiting her Grandmother in Buenos Aires when she was a young child. She spoke in detail about how her Grandmother would go every Thursday to join one of the most famous pressure groups of the modern age. The Mothers of the Disappeared. The Mothers of the *Plaza de Mayo* were an association of women who had lost children and grandchildren to the Dirty War, began calling international attention to the plight of the "desaparecidos" (disappeared persons). There were weekly Thursday afternoon vigils in the *Plaza de Mayo* in front of the presidential palace. Lorena's own mother joined her whenever she was in Buenos Aires and when the children were old enough, she would take them too.

They would sit and listen and offer support to these valiant women who just wanted answers and to know what had happened to their children, husbands, brothers and sisters and grandchildren.

As a treat for good behaviour, they would then take the children to Café Tortoni, established in 1858. Lorena spoke of it with awe. She described the stiff and disapproving suited staff, who sneered at all who had the audacity to set foot over the threshold. Paintings covered the walls and there was a magnificent stained glass ceiling. The counter was so highly polished that you could see your reflection in the wood and the till was a work of mechanical genius with elaborate keys all finished in brass. Lorena giggled as she recounted the joy of being served an Alfajor—a chocolate coated sandwich biscuit which came in a gold foil wrapper. She went on to explain that the café was equally as famous for its tango performances but this was something that she never attended. Lorena left on a two week trip around the UK soon after our lunch in search of all the walls, rocks and stones that had so caught her attention in her geography lessons at school. She was delighted by the thought that the English had built a wall to keep the Scots out and that the Irish had a stone that you had to kiss upside down while leaning over vertical drop and which then gave you the magical powers of "The gift of the gab". Huge slabs of rock that peoples had danced around at summer solstice in the most pagan of rituals and which lined up on one day of the year, held a degree of romance and excitement for her and millions of others.

Bates, Bell, Buss, Dexter, Langridge, Shaw, Suttle and Thomson

15 June – 11st 2 – BP 90/65
Late May/Early June 1995

I did miss her during those two weeks. Her youth and vibrancy and her enquiring mind coupled with her desire to laugh was very apparent by its absence due to the silences which I had to endure while I drank my coffees. I questioned my feelings; I wasn't in love with her though I did feel a tremendous amount of affection for her, like you might do for a younger sister or a niece. I realised at this point that she was probably about the same age as Denis's daughter, who was my blood relation but whose name I didn't recall and who lived I did not know where.

I enjoyed Lorena's enthusiasm for life and her undaunted attitude to take off to a far flung and in her fellow countrymen's eyes, a hostile country and get entirely involved in our way of life. This must cause her parents some degree of trepidation and concern and I wondered if I ought to write to them and let them know that I was keeping an eye on their precious daughter. No sooner had I had this thought that I realised that I had an over inflated view of myself as their daughter was an independent young woman in charge of her own destiny and other than a few chats; I wasn't exactly keeping an eye on her. I pondered then if this would have sounded slightly sinister and instantly dismissed the thought from my mind.

One evening after work, few days after our lunch together, I sat down about to read the paper but I suddenly recalled the fact that Frederick Rubio had been involved in medical research and while it was something that held no interest to Lorena, I was truly intrigued to know more about what he had been involved in. As I have said before, these were the days before Google was a common feature in every household. I pondered the issue; it seemed an insurmountable quest to unravel as I didn't have very much to go on. I picked up some of my old medical books and looked through the index sections to see if the name Dr Frederick Rubio happened to jump out.

I drew a blank and then tried cross referencing against work done in Paraguay, Argentina and then expanded it to the whole of South America. I pondered the time frame that his work would have been conducted in and reckoned that the period of the 1930s to the 1970s. Again this was a haphazard guess from what Lorena had told me. I knew that her grandparents were both now dead. I finally decided to write to the British Medical Council and ask their archiving team if they would be kind enough to undergo a search through their records to see what this unearthed. I felt faintly embarrassed by my lack of information and real relevance. I was clearly exploiting my position as a doctor and wasting the valuable time of others to indulge my own idle curiosity. I fully expected either no reply at all or a strongly worded note, telling me not to waste other people's time.

I went to the local library the following Saturday and spend a few hours hunting through micro film records but again drew blanks. It was with some surprise then that at the end of afternoon surgery on the Monday, Sarah gave me a message from a nice sounding lady called Ursula Hutt from the BMC archives department.

'Oh, really? What did she say?' I was fully expecting some unpleasant stop wasting our time sort of message.

'She said that they had done their best with the information you had given them but it was like trying to find a needle in a hay stack. She said that she has popped a couple of articles and papers in the post to you and did say that if you wanted to get in touch with her directly, she could discuss what you are looking for in more detail. I have her extension number here.' Wow! This was a turn up for the books. I couldn't wait to see what she had found for me to read and whether or not it would answer my query about Frederick's research.

Sure enough the articles turned up in the post the following day. I saved opening Ursula's treasure trove until after evening surgery and armed with my glass of red, settled myself down. The articles were accompanied by a polite note, apologising for the lack of cohesive articles and urging me to contact Ursula if she could be of further assistance.

I spread the contents out in front of me and started to read. There was nothing that was attributed to Frederick Rubio, however, in one small article he was mentioned as an associate and collaborator to one H Gregor, who appeared to have done extensive work and research into genetics, though surprisingly, he was a vet. Startled by this revelation, what on earth was a vet doing in the field of medicine and more to the point, why was a doctor working with a vet in the field of veterinary medicine? This had to be part of a research program into genetic mutations and the trials were being done on pigs or monkeys. Though the papers I read and the articles were of interest, there was very little that linked them to either Frederick or Gregor. Paraguay seemed to be the link to the information received and after I had read through, I felt strangely disappointed.

What on earth did I expect? At least I now thought I knew what Grandfather Rubio had been researching. Genetics is a deeply complex and broad field and extremely interesting. Research projects take years to harbour results and I wondered if Frederick had ever achieved success. I decided that I had probably wasted enough of my time and Ursula's. I would ask Sarah tomorrow to drop her a quick note and thank her on my behalf for her efforts. It gnawed away at me and I knew I would not rest until I had some better answers. It wasn't important but I couldn't bear the not knowing.

But why was Frederick working with a vet on a genetics program? What had he been trying to cure? What hereditary conditions had he been trying to correct and why in Paraguay? Why couldn't he do his research in Argentina? Maybe he knew Gregor and had gone to him, why would a doctor go to a vet? Why not the other way round? Which way round was it? A doctor assisting a vet on a veterinary program or a vet and doctor working with animals to find a cure to a human medical condition? I realised that I had made the assumption that they were working on the latter, surely a doctor working in the field of veterinary research would be about as much use as a chocolate teapot. What on earth had they been up to? How could they bring anything to each other's fields? A million whys swirled around in my head and none of them appeared to have an answer. It then struck me that Gregor didn't sound like a Spanish name either. I decided that another visit to the library was called for at the weekend to see if I could find out anything further about Gregor?

I had known a vet when I was younger. I had never met someone in such bad health. Bruises that covered his body that you couldn't believe didn't come from some violent fight. He was perpetually exhausted through lack of sleep as a result of being called out at all hours. They say that doctors are married to their work, vets I think breathe their work. I wonder if he ever had the nervous breakdown that for so long I suspected he would have.

I had to put my library trip on hold for a few weeks.

Bates, Bell, Buss, Dexter, Lenham, Oakman, Parks, Shaw, Suttle and Thomson

July – Breathless, Cramp, Uncontrollable Bouts of Panic and Unease June 1995

Lorena returned from her whirlwind tour of the British Isles and was full of enthusiasm for all that she had seen and the people who she had met. Barely pausing to draw breath, she would go from one adventure story to another, relaying every single fact about where she had been at an astonishing speed. I noted that although her English had improved immeasurably, her ability to articulate deteriorated as her excitement levels rose. More than once I had to tell her to slow down. Still, it did fill me with pleasure to see such animation on such a joyful and innocent face. I had absolutely no interest whatsoever in the places she had visited but could not help being captivated by her delight. She had drunk Guinness in Ireland and informed me as if I didn't already know that you had to say, Slancha. She had walked in the footsteps of giants, had danced in the pubs to the sounds of the man on the fiddle and proudly showed me her Arran jumper. 'The pattern is very important, you know, because the fishermen would wear the jumpers and if a body washed up on the beaches after a violent Atlantic storm, they would be able to identity it by the pattern on the jumper.' *Clearly a sales pitch for the gullible tourist*, I thought to myself. She had drunk Whiskey in Scotland and had got involved with highland dancing, partaken of haggis and been horrified by an orange drink called Irn Bru. I shuddered when she described the deep fried mars bars. She had been up before dawn to watch the sun rise up over Stonehenge along with many others, who a couple of times a year became pagan worshipers. She proudly announced that she was reading Daphne Du Maurier's Jamaica Inn after visiting the wilds of Devon and Cornwall.

She informed me that she was off again at the end of the month to try to see some more of Europe and she expected to be gone for a couple of months before returning to England. She was undecided at this point whether or not she would go straight home from here or if she would work up until the start of the European winter season and do another winter of ski teaching.

I felt saddened to hear that someone of whom I knew relatively so little, was such a small part of my world and who really had no bearing on my life but who at the same time I knew so much about had become one of the greatest parts of my life and who had altered my thoughts and viewpoints on so many aspects was soon to no longer be a part of my day to day being. I mentally shock myself and pulled myself together. *Enjoy the opportunities we had to chat and make the most of our discussions*, I told myself. I squeezed every last moment I could out of our coffee chats and would impatiently glare at people who needed serving by Lorena and who took her time away from me. By now I had a very clear idea about her family, life and thoughts and views on most aspects of our world. I relished her enthusiasm and adventurous spirit, her desire to absorb as much as she could about the world and people around her and any thought or culture alien to her own.

I offered to accompany her to a day at the races. She was delighted at the prospect and at the appointed hour. I collected her and escorted her to Goodwood Races. Goodwood is a huge estate. In 1802, the third Duke of Richmond introduced horse racing there to entertain army officers. Later on in 1914, the sixth Duke of Richmond added golf to the estate and the airfield there went in just after the war in 1948, built by The Earl of March. I had managed to find an appropriate suit, which was slightly out of vogue and had certainly seen better days but a final inspection in the mirror satisfied me that I wouldn't make us a laughing stock. I finished off my look with a straw hat. It was the first time I had seen her in anything other than jeans. In heels and a floaty dress, which a touch of make-up, made her almost unrecognisable and possibly one of the most stunning women I had ever set eyes on. Her elegant posture and luscious hair added to the picture, making her seem almost regal. She was delighted by the effort I had made and curtseyed to me. I ignored her silliness and opened the car door for her to get in.

We managed to position ourselves at the finishing post and admired each and every horse and rider who went past. The garishly bright colours of the jockeys silks against the gleaming coats and flaring nostrils of these finely muscled beasts was quite a mesmerising vision, only bettered by the sight of them pounding along on the turf. As they cantered up to the starting line, we would rush to the betting booths and place on our bets. A pound each way as Lorena was trying to save money. These were strict rules that I imposed at the beginning. Clearly her ability to spot a winner based on bright colours and hideously elaborate names was far better than my own and by the end of the day she had won a princely 75 pounds against my 14 pound loss. She was tickled pink and on such a high that she danced all the way back to the car, drawing stares of admiration from the male audience and glares of what I can only assume was envy and jealousy from the females. I had never been interested in social events and certainly not horse racing but I had to acknowledge to myself, it was one of the most pleasurable days I could remember having ever.

She reciprocated my invitation to the races with one of her own. She wanted to go to the British Museum and Natural History Museum. She caught me out, the thought of the underground, all the people, the pushing and shoving, sweaty strangers in close confines, the standing, the public transport, I found I couldn't bear the thought of it more than I wanted to spend a day with Lorena. I regretfully declined and realised that my own insular world of comfort and familiarity had spoilt me for adventure and my horror of crowds that I had developed after my accident really hadn't diminished over the years. She didn't seem remotely offended and happily took off on her own to London and more adventures.

I had invited her to come to my flat over the surgery when she returned for a glass of wine, so that she could tell me all about her day and what she had seen and learnt. She arrived shattered but exhilarated and as I sat back with my glass of Argentinean red, I admired the glow in her face and her sparkling eyes. It was as before she fired off facts about blue whales, ancient Egyptians, stone-age tools, Greek artefacts found in far flung areas of modern day Afghanistan. She intently relayed facts to me about the Silk Road and how in China there is a village of tall red heads with curly hair and marked Roman noses. After 30 minutes of her incessant fact flinging, I found myself entirely bemused and having lost track of the conversation as we raced from one subject to another. Just before 10 pm, she looked at her watch and proclaimed that she was meeting a friend and they were going out dancing, so she had to dash.

After she left, I decided to finish what was left in the bottle and considered the enthusiasm and energy of youth. I wasn't that old myself, only 50 this year but as a result of the crash followed by years of pain and long hours of work, not to mention my heartbreak from my failed marriage, which never left me, I felt very much older and physically, emotionally and mentally more broken than my fellow age group. *I wondered if I had always been old before my time had my crash stolen more from me than just my skill at cricket and what I now saw as my youth?* Dancing goodness, what a horrific thought. I drained my glass and grumpily stared at the now empty bottle. I then looked up at my trophy, normally this made me feel better but tonight it just looked like a cheap tacky trinket.

Bates, Bell, Buss, Dexter, Langridge, Lenham, Oakman, Parks, Suttle and Thomson

Cramp, Tired, Terrible Dreams, Balance Very Bad

Lorena left in early July with the friend with whom she had travelled around the British Isles and gone dancing with a jolly Dutch girl, called Heidi with a face like an Edam cheese and two enormous long blond plats either side of her head, exactly how a Heidi should look in my view from the romantic childhood story of a Swiss girl with the same name. I made Lorena promise me that she would send me a post card from each destination so that I could plot her progress around Europe. I delighted in and greedily enjoyed every postcard and impatiently waited for the next to arrive. Paris, Monte Carlo, Barcelona, Seville, Porto, Rome, Florence, Venice, Zurich, Vienna, Prague, Strasburg, Lichtenstein and Berlin; the cards came thick and fast, all written with the same level of excitement and pleasure in her surroundings. I could hear her voice as I read each one and had invested in some fridge magnets so that I could see all the cards at the same time. "Such a beautiful place", "Fantastic People", "You would love this", "Wonderful food", "Oh my, the museums are incredible", "Such an amazing adventure", "Better than I could imagine", I noted that too many more cards and I'd have to find a new way of displaying them all as I was running out of space.

There were no more cards after the one from Berlin. After a week I started to worry and after two weeks, I considered contacting Interpol. Realising that this would be utterly preposterous; she was entitled to send postcards to whom, whenever and wherever she choose. Maybe there was a postal strike or she was so far flung that they didn't sell postcards. Still, the worry would not leave me and each day I asked Donatella if she had heard anything. Donatella had no more news than I did and regarded me with a mixture of sly mirth and friendly concern.

'Doctor, you must not worry, she is young; she is having fun. If you want to worry, you should look at my legs, these varicose veins, oh, Doctor and how they hurt me!' She wailed. I was very familiar with Donatella's varicose veins and had told her that really she needed surgery. She would not entertain this as it meant that she would be unable to work for several weeks and would have to rest with her feet up. In her opinion, the café would come to a grinding halt if she wasn't there to oversee things and, therefore, she would go on suffering and to my irritation not in silence. One day, I bad-temperedly snapped,

'Donatella, I will not have this discussion with you again, you know what you need to do and, frankly, I think you are being reckless with you narrow-minded attitude.' It took a lot to stop Donatella in her tracks but that did it. The look of hurt confusion on her face made me realise that perhaps I had used a little bit too much force in my voice. I wished her a good day and turned around and left the café before she could irritate me further and I could cause more upset.

My run in with Donatella was on a Saturday morning and to cool off, I took myself to the library and started to research Grandfather Rubio's friend, Gregor. It really didn't take me long to discover far more about him that I could ever have wanted to know. The reading left me feeling distinctly unwell and the enormity of who he was and the implications of Frederick Rubio's relationship with him became blindingly obvious.

As I sat there, confused and bewildered by what I had found, it struck me that sometimes ignorance is bliss and there are occasions whereby the past really is better left alone. Once you learn a fact, you cannot then claim ignorance and if the fact is upsetting or disturbing, then that is your burden to carry and deal with. There is a marked difference between the need to know and the want to know and when you want to know, you rarely consider the implications of how you will deal with the knowledge you have just sought out. A position I was now in and struggling to cope with. By our nature humans are naturally curious creatures but I think we rarely consider the full possible implications of any new information.

I then realised that I had gone behind Lorena's back and had unearthed the most horrific of secrets about her family, which would cause much pain and possibly damage. How on earth could I have betrayed her and would I ever be able to look her in the eye again, knowing now what I did about her grandfather and his activities? I left the library and found a public toilet where I vomited violently, I felt cold and sick inside. I was covered in cold sweat and felt distinctly shaky. My vision was not clear and I wondered if at any moment I may pass out. As I wandered blindly back home, I saw Frederick Rubio's cold menacing face and eyes and the fact that I had had such a strong reaction to his photo now made perfect sense.

I spent the next day in bed. I felt so ill but thankfully there was no one who I was answerable to as I couldn't even bring myself to think about what I had found out. By Monday morning surgery, I was composed again and had my professional venire back in place. I got through the week managing to block out my retched visit to the library. It was only on the Friday evening that I allowed myself to consider what I had found out, coupled with increasing anxiety as I had still not heard from Lorena. That last postcard had said that she was on her way to Poland and my imagination had by now considered every plausible mishap.

I pondered fact by fact from my research mission to the library. Helmut Gregor was a false name that a man by the name of Josef Mengele had adopted on his passport that he had used to escape from Europe in the late 1940s and then returned to Europe in the mid-1950s to marry his dead brother's wife. He was originally from Germany and had been infamously known as Auschwitz's Angel of Death. A doctor who performed unimaginable experiments on children and adults as part of Hitler's quest to create a superior race. Genetic engineering in modern day terms to you and me but known as Eugenics.

What did this mean from Lorena's family's point of view? Frederick Rubio must have been known what Mengele was up to? Rubio himself was a doctor and I already knew that he was involved in genetic research. Therefore, logic dictated that he must have been involved in similar experiments as were suggested by the documented evidence which had been emerging from first-hand accounts that continued to pour out from victims and their families, who were subjected to the horrors of the Nazis. I tried to separate the emotion from the facts. It was too easy to assume any number of scenarios and I decided that for my own peace of mind, I had to do some more reading on the subject and attempt to build a more accurate picture on the subject. I would go to Waterstones tomorrow and get some books to broaden my education on the matter.

Bates, Bell, Buss, Dexter, Lenham, Oakman, Parks, Suttle and Thomson

Late July/Early August

I had to drive to our nearest town of note, which ironically is a city on account of it having a cathedral, an antiquated and redundant form of classification in our modern day world but equally delightful and unique to our nation. I had always looked forward with a degree of excitement to going to bookshops, either new or second-hand ones. I wandered into Waterstones the next day with a huge sense of guilt hanging over me. To dread going to a place, that was my Mecca or Holy Grail, was a new and entirely contradictory feeling for me. I felt sure that I must stand out as a man with a guilty secret, a man who knew more than he should and therefore was guilty of crimes by association. I found the section on military history easily and was dismayed to see how much had been written about wars that went back it seemed before time had begun. What possessed us to fight so prolifically and with such ferocity and disregard for life? It seemed that each war evolved on from the previous one with an even greater ability to violently kill and maim more people and cause an increasing amount of horror.

As a race, I am staggered by our ability to move on and recover from our own depravity and as one who has dedicated my life to assisting others to be well in theirs, the fact that there is a whole psyche in existence that aims to wipe out and decimate people in the name of greed, religion, race, creed or just being on the wrong side of the fence disgusts me to such an extent that in my darker moments, I wonder about the futility of life as we know it. The ultimate good versus evil, millennia long battle which appears to get no closer to being won. I suppose though that if we throw in our hats and give up, we are then defeated and I'm not convinced as humans we are programmed to accept defeat. Is this what the Chinese consider to be Yin and Yang, the fact that we must have balance and one force cannot exist without the other? With peace we must have war? And then the cycle begins again?

I felt a huge sense of disgust at the project that I had set myself but at the same time, burying my head in the sand and pretending it didn't happen surely made me guiltier, guilty of disregard, ignorance and not caring. Surely knowledge gives us the tool to educate ourselves, move forwards and to learn? I didn't know and stopped my internal struggles and started looking in earnest. I finally selected a book on the Nazis and their crimes and another on how the Nazis escaped prosecution after the war ended. I managed to find a book on Mengele and I also acquired a book on Argentina and their acceptance of Nazi war criminals. They were hard back books with glossy covers that could be removed and once purchased this, I did instantly and threw the covers in a bin. I was left with dark backed books which would look innocently like any other tone. I didn't want Mrs Miller or worse Lorena when she returned if she returned to see what I had been reading. I would keep my guilty learning as I now regarded it to myself.

Over the next fortnight I would read into the early hours of the morning about what had happened under the Nazi regime in concentration camps and who, some of the main protagonists, were how they escaped Europe at the end of the war and who they escaped from, who helped them and where they went.

If I'm honest, even as a doctor, who is familiar with all sorts of medical conditions and the inner workings of the human body, the way disease and illness manifests itself and the resulting aliments and side effects on the human body, most of which are extremely unpleasant. I cannot bring myself to even attempt to commit to this memory, the horrors and blatant depravity of the first-hand accounts and cold-blooded (pardon the pun) factual accounts of the "research" experiments that took place under the Nazi regime. It left me feeling so shaken and bemused by what I read that I could not comprehend from my own perspective as one, who has done the very best that I can to alleviate the suffering of others, promote health and wellbeing and where I cannot fix the aliment and consequential symptoms and outcomes that I have always endeavoured to provide a stable and balanced perspective and provide calm to those facing their own destiny.

These demons, who performed agonising and fatal experiments in the name of research and science, which I suppose one could argue that there was an element of this, though it is questionable but in such barbaric and pointless manners, without care or compassion for their prey, who were no different to themselves but whom found themselves the victims of a circumstance over which they had no control, appalled me and disturbed me to such an extent that I wondered how much as men we really know our own kind. Surely, these fascist bastards were in fact an evidence of a less obvious experiment that too much liberty and power rots basic human values and leads to a return of almost caveman like behaviour. I'll take what I want, when I want and how I want because I want and you can't stop me because I'm stronger than you. The fuck you, I'm alright school.

I suppose, as a child at school, I knew the basic facts about the Second World War; it was modern and very recent history. When I was growing up, no one didn't have a story from their own family or friends about a love one lost and the hardships that impacted on our lives for many years after the end of the war but like so many events that shake our modern day world, we become immune to the reality. Earth shattering facts that become idol chat and somehow we grow a protective skin that stops us from really considering what is going on around us. We zombie walk through the most shocking of events and just carry on. I can honestly say now, looking back that as a youth and young man, I was far more concerned with my own brilliance than by the rationing and horrific stories from the war. They were inconveniences and minor details in my own march forwards. I remember seeing wounded, disfigured and maimed men, shuffling along with crazed or vacant looks in their eyes, too broken and traumatised to describe their experiences while continually reliving the horrors in their minds, driving them to the point of despair. I completely disregarded them and what they had gone through as they were such a common sight and at that age, I simply didn't care. Their untold hell for their countrymen's liberty turned them either into objects of shame or mockery. Shame now flooded me. Now I took this opportunity to plug some of the gaps in my knowledge about who and what the Nazi's were. It is too enormous a subject to even attempt to fully grasp, so for the purposes of my own research, I stuck to the details and personalities, who were most relevant to my own area of research.

Since my research in the mid-1990s, there have been many new developments as more and more information has poured out about this particular aspect of history but I will focus on the information that I had at my disposal at the time as this subject is so vast and complex.

Bates, Bell, Buss, Dexter, Lenham, McCarthy, Oakman, Parks and McCarthy

August 2016

A war that claimed over 60 million lives of which over six million Jews were murdered by the Nazis and many of the perpetrators escaped scot free to live in countries such as America, Canada and South America, where they took on new identities. Some were later tracked down and prosecuted but most lived and died through to old age as free men. The lists of who the main criminals were are well-documented, in fact most infamous culprits are far better known than the hundreds of thousands of selfless people, who worked tirelessly to undo and minimise the horrors these beasts unleashed.

I found the history to the war to be deeply complex but I have simplified it with no intent of disrespect of the facts but for my own inability to comprehend all of what took place. I read that after the fall of the Axis Alliance, which was made up of Germany, Italy and Japan in 1945 by which time the key protagonists were already dead, such as Hitler and Mussolini. These figure heads were a symbolism but many people such as Josef Mengele "The Angel of Death" at Auschwitz and his colleagues, Adolf Eichmann, Franz Stangl, dubbed "The Architect of the Holocaust" and Ante Pavelic were still very much alive. With the right connections it seems, as is so often the way, they were able to evade the trials at Nuremberg by escaping from Europe through a system of established routes known as the "Nazi Ratlines".

These were routes set up by sympathetic parties, where a blind eye was turned and in the chaos of the aftermath of the war many played dumb to the authorities about who they were helping cross borders and escape to new lives in exchange for lucrative backhanders.

Spain had largely remained neutral throughout the war but to its shame, assisted with the transferal of many of these criminals, who had crossed into its territories and on to South America, making Spain a de facto supporter of the Axis Alliance. Was their own civil conflict a cause for this attitude? I was staggered to read that the Swiss were some of the worst of the lot. Again remaining neutral throughout the war, the Swiss offered a first class route out of the "hot zone" for these criminals and their collaborators and offering anonymity, the whole way to freedom, principally into Italy.

Not only had the Swiss assisted with the hiding of millions of dollars of artefacts, gold and bullion stolen from innocent Jews, who were then generally sent on to concentration camps but they adopted an attitude of silence and secrecy about these matters for decades after the events in question. The question of large scale money laundering is one of serious consequence, which rumbles on today under the description of Nazi Gold.

Italy was a hot bed of activity for the Nazi ratlines, Mussolini was its fascist leader and it is the home of the Catholic Church, whose role here was beyond contempt. This institution which proclaimed to protect and preserve the word of God, our Father, could not have been more ungodly if it had tried. Not only did they deliberately look the other way to the murder of millions but they actively protected their murderers, thus denying justice for the innocent victims of these crimes. Their actions were carried out under the weak and pathetic excuse of the fear of the spread of communism but what can only amount to being the act of fascist support. I read more than one account that the Catholic Church was paid most royally to look the other way and the coffers at the Vatican were full to bursting with Nazi loot. As I read these countless facts again and again, I felt the sands shifting under my feet. I was born in The Republic of Ireland and like all of my fellow countrymen, I was brought up a Catholic. I attended a Catholic school run by monks and was indoctrinated in the Catholic way of thinking. To discover to such an extent that they were as a collective, frauds left me reeling and questioning my own identity and beliefs. I do hasten to add here that after I left my school days behind me, I failed spectacularly with attending mass as I had always regarded it as a bit of a chore. However, as with many organisations, while the top and key players are invariably corrupt, the lowly and faithful carry out good works. I could think of so many loyal church volunteers who selflessly gave up hours of their time to good causes and who were unshakable in their faith and beliefs. In the 1980s, various stories about abuse within the Catholic Church started to emerge and these events continue to haunt the church to this day.

Gazing up at my trophy I dissected the sheer scale of the atrocities and death of the Second World War. It was appalling and yet had we in any way become a better people and learnt anything through this experience? The hatred still existed, the bitterness was greater, and distrust knew no bounds. The killing has not ceased. Every day we read about or hear on the news that so many have been killed in the Middle-East between Jews and Muslims, Muslims and Muslims, Northern Ireland between the Protestants and Catholics, clashes in Asia between Buddhists and Muslims, fighting in Africa between tribes, between the Russians and Afghans, between Pakistanis and Indians, intolerances between different branches of what amounted to the same faith in The United States. Yet, nowhere does any faith encourage the destruction and violence towards other faiths. Isn't the message to live in peace with your fellow men and respect each man's beliefs? Will we ever find any kind of peace and respite for our fellow men or are we just programmed to fight? It does still fill me with a sense of horror though that we hear that 20 are killed in a car bomb and dozens are injured one day, then the next we hear that 50 are killed in a stampede and many are rushed to hospital. Then the next a hospital is the target of an attack and unknown numbers are dead. Then the next a deranged gunman has gone on a killing spree in a school and we will bring you the latest update when we know the final death toll. And day in and day out, we are continually assaulted by these horror stories and we take them for granted, never once stopping to consider the impact each event must be having on the individuals involved and their loved ones and how their lives have been senselessly ended or distorted forever. Despair and grief at it all filled me.

Bates, Bell, Buss and Dexter

August 1995

Bishop Alois Hudal, an Austrian, assisted Eichmann and Stangl in helping war criminals to escape. Hudal would vouch to the forged identities of the escapees and used the Red Cross to obtain papers for these men. In return he was handsomely rewarded with ill-gotten booty. I read that it is reported that Hudal assisted Stangl to get a job in Damascus, a man who had committed over one million murders in Austria.

Another horror from within the Catholic Church was a Croatian Bishop, Monsignor Krunoslav Draganovic a supporter of the Ustashe, the Croatian Nazi army. The leader of the Ustashe was one Ante Pavelic who was quite possibly one of the worst men within the Nazi regime and who prided himself on his ability to outdo the SS in terms of brutality and cruelty. This was aimed towards Serbs, Jews and Gypsies and they were slaughtered in their hundreds of thousands. This lunatic escaped to Argentina curtesy of Monsignor Kruoslav Draganovic. To say that Monsignor Krunoslav Draganovic was able to get his sticky stained fingers on the Ustashe loot would not be an understatement and he also assisted Klause Barbie, "The Butcher of Lyon" evade capture in France with the full co-operation of American officials. So you see, the web of corruption and disregard for another's actions in the name of personal gain is global. Greasing the palm in exchange for looking the other way.

So why did Argentina let the Nazis in, I pondered? They were thousands of miles away and at face value well and truly out of things as they had also apparently remained neutral throughout the war. It seems that at the end of the war, Argentina had a German population of about 250,000, so was it pressure from within? Possibly this was a factor. However, there was a non-extradition agreement with the Allied countries and Perón who was the president at the time was an admirer of the Axis Alliance and in particular Nazi Germany. Why? In case they needed assistance from their big bad neighbour, who frequently liked to interfere in other countries internal affairs. The United States of America. The USSR was a growing power and sending some frightening ripples around the world, so again keeping the Axis Alliance and especially the Germans on side was not a bad strategy in their view. In 1943, Perón visited Germany in all probability to negotiate an arms deal with them and it is believed that after the war ended, many German Nazis actually held positions within the Perón Government after 1946. It does not take a genius to conclude that this would have helped the emigration of many of their own kind into Argentina.

Once in the receipt of a landing permit and visa on arrival in Argentina, many went on to obtain high ranking jobs. As many of them came with illegally acquired wealth, stolen from their victims. This was then invested into their new homeland. Perón was very keen to acquire as much German technology as he could, some of which was developed during the war, hence another reason for his welcoming approach.

An interesting fact though is that under the Perón open door policy, Argentina accepted more Jewish immigrants than any other country on that continent and today has the sixth largest Jewish population anywhere in the world. It is believed by some that he genuinely sympathised with the Jews and their treatment at the hands of the Nazis and as well as Nazi criminals. Perón also employed many Jews in his government. I couldn't help but speculate that this may have had more to do with their well-known business acumen and financial successes. So it seems that under Perón, Argentina cast aside the politics and hatred of others and welcomed all who could help them prosper. I wondered whether the ethics here were questionable which they undoubtedly were but the more I thought about it, the more this seemed a remarkably pragmatic approach from the Argentinean government's point of view. Who knows?

Bates, Bell, Buss, Dexter, Lenham, Oakman, Parks, Suttle and Thomson

Mid to late August 1995

A letter addressed to me in handwriting with which I had become familiar sat on Sarah's desk, waiting for me. I snatched it up and tore it open, anxious to know what it said. It was a very brief note.

'Dear, Doctor (no matter how often I asked her to call me James, she insisted on calling me doctor). I write this because I know you are worry for me. Something very bad has happened, I am okay and I come back soon. I think I really need your help.

Lorena.'

I didn't know what on earth to make of that! Something bad had happened but she was okay. That was almost worse than not knowing. Still she was alive and was coming back soon. With that I had to content myself.

Lorena didn't materialise until the following week. I had just settled down with a very full glass of red and a combination of the papers, a medical journal, which had come in the post that day and a text book on skin disorders, a patient had presented themselves earlier with some very unpleasant looking sores and while I thought I knew what it was, I did just want to check that I hadn't overlooked anything more obvious. The phone rang and although I was tempted to ignore it, I hadn't had a sip of wine yet, so obligingly got up and answered it. It was very hard to understand the person who was on the other end and what on earth they were saying. I only knew one person, who could speak so hysterically and after I shouted at her to shut up and answer my questions, I established from Donatella that Lorena had returned and was seriously unwell. I told her that I would be there in five minutes. I gathered up my Gladstone bag, which always lived by the front door overnight in case of an emergency, such as this. It was a habit of many years and one that had served me very well on several occasions.

Donatella lived in the road behind her café and Lorena lived with her, after all she was family. The door was open and Donatella's diminutive husband, George, was hovering anxiously on the threshold looking out. He seemed to relax once he saw me and said that he was just popping out and would leave me to it. It was no secret that George drank far more than was good for him but he had my sympathies living with Donatella. He was clearly running off to the pub.

With no one to guide me, I headed up the stairs as I could hear voices coming from one of the rooms there. I knew my way around reasonably well as Donatella's varicose veins had resulted in more than one house call over the years.

Following the voices, I walked into the bedroom where Lorena was curled up in a ball on the bed and Donatella was fussing over her. I insisted that Donatella go downstairs and make us tea, one with lots of sugar in for Lorena. I shut the bedroom door behind her and turned to look at Lorena. She was staring into space, her eyes were glazed over and she seemed trapped in a world of her own. I saw instantly that the lovely slim girl was now little more than a bag of bones, her once unblemished skin looked dull and her glossy hair was far from that now. I drew up a chair next to the bed and reached out for Lorena's hand. It was like holding something lifeless and so cold. I squeezed her hand gently as she was not responding to my voice and slowly her eyes focused on me. I squeezed her hand again, nothing more. I tried this a couple more times in a regular sequence and after a moment or two, I detected the slightest of pressure. I carried on with this and slowly she started to respond. There was no point in asking her what the matter was; clearly whatever it was, she was incapable of telling me but which each slightly stronger squeeze, she was able to communicate that she knew I was there and that she was returning back into the room with me. We remained like this with no words spoken until Donatella erupted back into the room and shattered the peace. I let go of Lorena's hand and slowly while supporting her rigid body, I eased some more pillows behind her head so that she was in a more upright position. I sent Donatella off in search of hot water bottles and blankets. The girl was colder than a block of ice.

The tea was hot and shuddering sweet and slowly I managed to get Lorena to drink a few mouthfuls. I held the tea to her lips again and she shook her head. I ignored her and insisted that she drink more; it was only when she started to protest more strongly that I put the tea down. The fact that she was now responding and resisting was a good sign. Once I had her tucked up with blankets and a hot water bottle for her very cold hands, I offered her more tea.

'No, Doctor, no, are you trying to kill me?' she whispered. It was barely audible and I had to lean right forward to catch the words. The sudden and unexpected humour of her question caught me entirely off guard and made me laugh out loud. It sounded over loud in the stillness of the room. 'Donatella put a lot of sugar in, did she?' She hardly moved but I detected a nod. Glad to see a return to something close to my young friend. I instantly adopted my don't mess with me, I'm your doctor attitude and in a stern voice said,

'Right, young lady, I don't really know what the matter is but it seems to me you haven't been eating properly or taking care of yourself and you of all people should know better than that. So I am going to assume, based on your current state and your letter, that you have suffered some kind of shock. I am going to ask Donatella to bring you some soup, all of which you are going to eat and if you don't, I am going to have you admitted to hospital and have you wired up to a drip, do I make myself clear? You are also going to drink this glass of water and take this sedative. In the morning you are going to have some more tea, though maybe with slightly less sugar in and eat some dry toast and have a hot shower and a wash. If you fail to do any of this, there will be serious consequences and I will be very angry. Is that clear? Is that clear?' I repeated when she failed to answer me.

She meekly whispered, 'Yes.' I watched her swallow down a low dose of a muscle relaxant and went off to find Donatella and issued her with strict instructions regarding food and hydration. I insisted that she call me if things declined as I wasn't sure at this juncture just how serious matters were. However, I was reasonably confident that with common sense, Lorena would be physically fine. The dead look in her eyes were an entirely different matter but one thing at a time. My guilt overtook me as I couldn't help but wonder if the information about her grandfather that I had stumbled upon wasn't the same nasty shock that Lorena had encountered. After all, she had been going to Poland, Donatella called Sarah while I was dealing with my early morning appointments. By all accounts, Lorena had most of the minestrone soup last night and had slept peacefully. She had two cups of tea and half a slice of dry toast before heading off for a long hot shower this morning. All positive signs. I missed out my usual stop off at the café and went to see Lorena, who I was pleased to see was sat on the sofa with clean hair and clean clothes on. She was very shy and unwilling to maintain any eye contact with me. Donatella tactfully withdrew from the room and left us to it. It crossed my mind that the fact that Donatella was not at the café was in itself, an unheard of event and indicated how seriously concerned she was about Lorena's condition. Not even Donatella's varicose veins had kept her away from her beloved café ever. Even when I had to make house visits, which were always after closing time, to see her and repeatedly scolded her, telling her to keep her weight off her feet. I had even threatened not to visit her at home, saying if she was well enough to serve me my daily coffee, she was well enough to come to the surgery. Yet, somehow, I always visited her at her home.

I pulled up a chair next to the sofa and again reached out for Lorena's hand. At first she was very hesitant to hold my hand but then reluctantly placed her hand in mine. I noted that her body temperature was far better and although she looked pale and washed out, her skin looked far better than it had the night before. We didn't talk at all and this carried on for several days. Every time I visited, I would just sit with her, observing her but not pushing her. Donatella kept me updated with food and fluid intakes and although Lorena wasn't eating very much, it was enough to start to rebuild her strength. After five days of this, I felt that we now needed to start making a bit more progress.

'Look at me, Lorena,' I commanded.

'What happened?' I'm not sure if it was because of my own research into her grandfather and his contemporaries past but I suddenly asked,

'What have you found out?' Her eyes flew to mine; it was the first real eye contact that we had had.

'What do you mean?' she said hoarsely. Panic and alarm registered on her face.

'Tell me what happened.'

'I can't, it is so terrible. I can't tell you, Doctor.'

'Lorena, as both your doctor and your friend, you must tell me, otherwise nothing can be done and I won't be able to help you.'

'I don't think anyone can help me.'

'Well, that may be the case but we won't know until you tell me, then I can tell you, whether or not, there is help to be had.'

I reflected on this point that I had a lot of experience of telling people over the years that they couldn't help me and it was down to a couple of nurses who had seen me through my rehabilitation and who had got me walking and moving again that I was able to walk so well and live an independent life. I had regarded them as brutal thugs at the time, entirely devoid of humanity and caring, mercilessly making me do exercises and practice walking with sticks while I bellowed in pain and frustration. With retrospect they had clearly cared the most and given me back my life. I borrowed a couple of chapters from their books and indulged in some tough love.

I had a very strong suspicion that the cause of Lorena's problem was coming face to face with an unexpected and hideous truth. Had I not known what I did as a result of what you might call my snooping? However, well-intended, perhaps I would have taken a different tact but if the cause of this was in essence survivor guilt, it was not Lorena's guilt to suffer. What her grandfather had done had nothing to do with her and she needed to realise this, otherwise, this could wipe out her love of life and her youth. Having first-hand experience of this with my own misadventures caused I hasten to add by me and no-one else, I was determined that she would not make the misguided mistakes that I had.

'Lorena, the last postcard I had from you, you said that you were going to Poland. Tell me what happened in Poland to you that has caused you so much upset. Did someone hurt you? Tell me what happened.' She refused to make eye contact with me and I noticed that her hands were constantly fidgeting, picking at her nails and she was chewing the inside of her cheek. 'Talk to me, Lorena.' I prompted. Still nothing. I took hold of both of her hands in mine and said, 'Look at me.' Reluctantly after a few moments, she cagily raised her eyes to mine.

Taking a gamble I said, 'Did you find out something about someone that has upset you?' The look of horror on her face made me think that I had pushed things too far but maybe, in fact, I was on the right lines.

Back tracking slightly I said, 'Tell me about Poland, what are the people like? I don't know much about the country but the people I have met from there have always been delightful. I don't think that I would like their food though.' She looked at me blankly.

'Yes, they are nice people, I don't remember the food.'

'So tell me about the countryside. Is it like England?'

'It is very green in some places.'

'So where did you go?'

'I went to…'

'Yes?'

'I went to…'

In spite of myself, I blurted, 'Lorena, did you go to Auschwitz?'

That same look of horror on her face as if she were looking right at the devil.

Bates, Bell, Buss, Dexter, Lenham, Oakman, Parks, Suttle and Thomson

Late August or even Early September 1995

'I, I...'

'You did, didn't you? And I think that you found out something more horrible than you thought possible. Am I right?' She nodded.

'Oh, Doctor, it was so terrible; what those beasts did to so many innocent people and the children.' Tears were running down her face and small sobs were shaking her body. I got her a box of tissues and gave her a tissue to wipe her eyes and blow her nose. I have never had a strong stomach when it comes to snotty noses and I have boxes of tissues all around my surgery, so that I don't have to deal with such situations. I had to hunt a bit harder at Donatella's home.

'I have never been but I imagine that from what I have heard and read that it is a very moving and sobering experience. The things that happened there, I know from my...' I faltered, 'from reading were barbaric and inhuman.'

'Yes, Doctor, they were.' It was as if we had open up a dam. Suddenly, she started to talk in her classic way, barely pausing to draw breath in her passion and emotion, her spoken

English deteriorated drastically but it was more than clear what she was saying, so I didn't interrupt her but just let her keep talking. She described how she and Heidi had decided to go to pay respect to the millions massacred and to understand what had really gone on there. Heidi's family were Jewish on her mother's side of the family and therefore this made Heidi Jewish, though by all accounts, her upbringing was slightly lapsed in this regard.

She described the eerie silence and stillness of the place. The lack of birdsong and the chilling feeling of menace that enveloped the experience and the air hung heavy. The only thing that I could liken this experience to was that early in our marriage, Lizzie had talked me into a driving holiday in France. We were driving in thick fog and apart from the obvious concerns in this situation, I could feel the hair suddenly stand up on the back of my neck. I had felt very nervous and uncomfortable. Suddenly, there was a break in the fog and we drove past a sign telling us that were travelling through the fields of the Somme. I was so anxious to get away from that haunted place whose peace had been destroyed permanently by all that had gone on before.

Lorena explained that photos were not allowed at Auschwitz, though why on earth anyone would want to photo such a place I couldn't imagine. There was a guide who talked to them as they were walked around, who explained quite cold bloodily what took place, the numbers involved and the distorted ideology behind these acts.

Lorena said that the guide was very good and spoke in facts, most of which were hard to hear and caused considerable distress. After that, they were taken to the holocaust centre, a short distance away where they were free to spend some time in the visitor centre. Lorena told me that at this point she had a feeling which was a premonition that something very bad was about to happen. She explained that same cold feeling of dread that went through her and how her heart had started to beat so hard that it hurt and felt as if her whole head was beating to the erratic rhythm of her heart. She said that everything started to feel as if she were an onlooker and was watching this happen to someone else as if she were looking at and hearing everything from some distance away and as if it were coming down a tunnel. All contradictory but entirely normal feelings at such a time. I didn't let on that I was several steps ahead of her here. I didn't want to stop her narrative and I certainly was not ready to come clean about my own feelings of guilt about what I had done. She went on to explain about the care and detail that was applied to the visitors centre, the information and the displays in the glass cabinets. Some personal effects found, old black and white photos. There were descriptions, both first hand and general about who was there and what happened. There were log books of the arrivals and those who were sent to the gas chambers.

She then looked me square in the eye with a slightly defensive attitude and said, 'Did you know that they performed experiments on people there?' *Okay, here we go*, I thought.

'Yes, Lorena, I did know that.'

'Do you know what they did?'

'Only from what I have read.' She looked down. She clearly didn't know how to go on. Anxious not to lose the momentum I prompted her to continue. It was essential that we get this out in the open for her to even start process the facts and then in turn start to heal. I cast my mind back to lectures at medical school about counselling and I remembered listening to my father. I knew that you should never rush people who are unburdening and certainly never hurry them along but I felt sure that if Lorena didn't continue now, it could be a long time before we got this far again.

'Tell me, Lorena.' She took a deep breath as if she was about to dive under water and said, 'They had doctors there, who did experiments on people, many did not survive. They were horrible experiments.' Silence again. I genuinely didn't know how to move this point forwards. We sat in silence for what seemed like a long time but maybe was just a matter of a couple of minutes.

'One of the doctors there was…it was my grandfather!'

Bates, Bell, Buss, Cooper, Dexter, Langridge, Lenham, Oakman and Parks

September 1995

With this, Lorena disintegrated into tears and sobs so violent that her whole body jerked with each breath. She cried so much that I couldn't believe that she could keep going. The sound was of a wounded animal in agony. I gently wrapped my arms around her shoulders and did my best to sooth her. I couldn't have stopped this stem of emotion if I had tried, so I just let her cry, frustrated that there was nothing I could do. Sometime later, the crying had not abated at all and in fact she had started to become quite hysterical. I extracted myself from her and noticed that my left shoulder was soaked through. I reached for my bag and produced some sedatives, which I made her swallow down with a small sip of water. Gradually, she started to calm down and about 30 minutes later, the crying ceased altogether. Looking across at her, I noted that she had actually fallen asleep. I went to find Donatella and told her that we had made some progress but Lorena was very fragile and weak from the crying. I wanted Lorena to rest but it was very important that she have something to eat and drink when she woke up.

'I phoned my cousin. I told him I must speak to your wife. I told Lorena's mother, her baby needs her. She is sick and a mother should be with her child when she is sick. She is booking a flight; she will be here as soon as she can.' I glared at Donatella with such anger. Not only had she frightened the life out of Lorena's family, telling them that their beloved daughter, who was now thousands of miles away from home, was sick with what they didn't know, so would be imagining all sorts but Lorena would now have to face the people she loved the most with a truth that would surely destroy the family. Not only was she dealing with the guilt of the past but now she would have to the brave the guilt associated with whatever inevitable hurt was to come out from what she had discovered. Telling a stranger had been hard enough for her, to tell her mother a horrific truth about her mother's father. Well, that was just unimaginable.

I was about to give Donatella a very graphic piece of my mind, when it dawned on me, was I so furious with her because I wanted to be the one to rescue Lorena from her turmoil. I didn't want to share her and a mother's love would be so much greater than anything I could offer. Maybe Donatella was right. At a time like this, a mother's love was probably the best cure of all. I thought back to my accident. I did not remember much love from my parents but then I was totally absorbed by both the physical and mental pain I was in. I was in hospital for so many months that all I remember was pain.

Gruelling grinding pain, that was exhausting and debilitating. I was frequently driven mad by my pain, shouting and screaming. Unable to think and pleading for release. My parents were both medically trained that I suspect that they monitored my progress by facts and results. My own experience from my patients is that one in pain is not always the most receptive of individuals and tends to be bad tempered and will put up barriers around themselves that are very difficult to break down. The carer is often more wounded emotionally than the injured party. Hateful words are remembered more by those who hear them than by those who say them. It is only the love that they have for the afflicted person that protects the carer from the hurt caused by their loved one. I now realise that perhaps I was a very difficult and unlovely patient.

I looked at Donatella. I couldn't really fault her. She had acting out of concern, compassion and love and perhaps she was right. Lorena should be with her mother.

'Okay, Donatella, that is a good idea. I can make arrangements to collect Lorena's mother from the airport if you like. Let me know the flight details when you have them and I think perhaps we should not tell Lorena just yet. I think it would be best if Lorena and her mother are reunited here rather than the airport, it is more private.' She looked surprised at my mild tone, clearly my behaviour was quite predictable and she had been bracing herself for one of my tellings off. She nodded in agreement and went off to the kitchen to cook something tempting for Lorena.

I got a phone call later that evening from Donatella. She told me that Lorena had eaten a small bowl of pasta and some ice cream and was asking if I could visit her. Her mother had called just a short while ago and would be landing at Heathrow in two days. I jotted down the details and made a mental note to ask Sarah to reschedule my appointments for

Tuesday afternoon. I slipped on my jacket and walked down the road.

Lorena had recently had a shower; her long hair was damp and slicked back. Her face was puffy and swollen and her eyes were still very red and sore. She smiled apologetically at me without making eye contact. I crouched down in front of her and held her hands, forcing her to look at me.

'Lorena, please, look at me. You have nothing to feel guilty for and you should not be ashamed of anything. You did not do anything wrong. Please, I am your friend and I am here to help you. Don't feel that you can't look at me.' I wasn't really prepared for what happened next. Not being a particularly demonstrative person, I was out of my comfort zone, just saying that. She let out a cry and threw her arms around me in a very fierce embrace. As I wasn't expecting this, my face was crushed uncomfortably against the zipper on her jumper top and I felt entirely discombobulated by the event, uncertain of how to behave and respond. I slowly managed to disentangle myself from her embrace and went to sit down in the arm chair next to her chair. To my surprise, when I managed to look her in the eye, she was smirking at me.

'How do you say it? The table is upside down now.'

'I think you mean the tables have turned. There is no need to get clever with me,' I said this more sternly than I had intended but I could see that she hadn't taken offence.

'I think you know, Doctor. You know all of this before I even said anything.' I felt the blood starting to creep up to my face, my hands were cold and clammy at the same time. Now suddenly I couldn't look at Lorena. The tables had indeed been turned.

'It doesn't matter, Doctor, please don't feel bad. I feel bad enough for everyone. Maybe it is making it easier for me to tell you.'

'Tell me exactly how you found out about your grandfather.' She closed her eyes and let out a gentle sign. She stayed like that for a moment or two as if she were bracing herself. When she opened her eyes again, she started to speak. 'There was a display with a photo of Mengele and a description of what he was doing, his experiments and those who performed these with him. I was reading so deeply that I didn't see the photo until I reached the end of the text. Before I saw the photo, I suddenly felt very odd, my heartbeat in my ears was so loud and I had the trembles. It was the same photo that I have, the one I showed you. So you see, there is no doubt it was him. He worked very closely with Mengele, I think that he was his protégé from what I could understand. He documented everything and helped Mengele to perform and record his experiments. His real name was Frederick Rubens. He changed it to Rubio when he escaped Europe and came to Argentina.'

'Oh my God!' Her hand flew to her mouth and she looked at me in horror as a thought struck her.

'Do you know what *Rubio* means?' I shook my head. '*Rubio* means blonde.'

'If you say someone is *muy rubio,* it means that they are very fair.'

'The perfect Aryan you mean?'

'Yes,' she whispered. We sat for a moment thinking about the dreadful irony of this.

'How do you think he escaped?' I asked. Lorena scrunched up her face.

'I don't know. I know that many did escape, I think it said at the information centre but by that point, I couldn't see or think or do anything. I lied to Heidi, I feel very bad for that. I told her that I was too upset by everything that I was reading that I had to leave. It is sort of true, not for the reasons she thinks. The lady in the information centre said that it happens to a lot of people, some people faint and some people vomit.' I thought of my own similar reaction when I had found out.

'So we left. After that, I told Heidi that I wanted to travel alone. She was fine about it. She wanted to go to Scandinavia to see a friend in Denmark. I said that I had to come back here because Donatella needed me. I had to be away from Heidi. You know I was looking at her, thinking my grandfather killed your family and you are so lovely to me. You should hate me and spit in my face but I couldn't tell her the truth. It hurt me with my shame to look at her.'

'Oh, Lorena, my poor friend.'

'Do you understand why I did and what I did, Doctor? I am not proud of myself but I didn't know how to behave.'

'I do understand, Lorena, and I think that you did the right thing.' I didn't really know if there was a right way to behave in the circumstances.

'Oh, Doctor, what on earth will I do? How can I tell my mother and my family this terrible thing?'

'Do you need to tell them Lorena?' I asked.

'But, of course, I do. I cannot lie to them.' Technically I argued in my mind, she wouldn't be lying. It was more an omission but I did understand that she needed to tell her family and if the roles were reversed, well, there was no point in saying that as they weren't and I had no one to tell, so to speak.

Bates, Bell, Buss, Cooper, Dexter, Langridge, Oakman, Parks, Shaw, Suttle and Thomson

September 2016

I had a busy Monday, all Monday's are busy and by the time I popped in to see Lorena at the end of the day, I felt exhausted. My back ached and I was quite irritable. I noted though that Lorena looked brighter and was starting to regain a bit of her former spirit. I dithered about whether or not Donatella and I should tell her that her mother was coming tomorrow. In the end, the opportunity never presented itself to tell her, so it went unsaid.

As I drifted off to sleep that night, I thought about the lady who I was going to meet tomorrow. Mamma Mute with her petit frame and blond hair and different coloured eyes. The daughter of a monster but who herself was filled with love. I had no doubts or concerns about recognising her, though I did realise that I had no idea if she spoke any English. That could make for a long journey back home if we were destined to be sat in silence. All of the things that I had wanted to tell her about her daughter's current state, may well have to go unsaid. Oh, well, what will be, will be. That was a phrase that I had heard so often during my childhood, my own mother had always said that. It had driven me mad when I was younger as it seemed such a pointless thing to say but suddenly I appreciated and understood the wisdom of it.

Sarah had done an excellent job of rescheduling my appointments and there were not too many grumbles by all accounts. It would take me well over an hour to get to the airport and the flight was due in at 4.30 pm, allowing for time to park and unforeseen delays, I would have to leave at 3 pm to be on the safe side. Not surprisingly, there were several last minute emergencies that I had to deal with, all of which turned out not to be emergencies at all and I didn't end up leaving until nearly 3.45 pm. As I rushed into the arrivals hall, the first people were just starting to come through.

I hastily looked around the hall to make sure that there was not a small blond lady looking lost. Thankfully, there wasn't. As I started to scan the people coming through, I realised that although I knew what she looked like, she didn't have a clue what I looked like and I hadn't thought to bring a sheet of paper with her name on. As more and more people came through the double doors into the arrivals, I noted that the majority of them were all good looking, well-dressed and healthy looking individuals, all with their own sense of style and a confidence to them that I had noted in Lorena. My anxiety levels started to go up again when the doors closed and no petit blond ladies had materialised. Had I got the wrong flight details? Had she missed the flight? Had I missed her coming through? I looked anxiously around the now heaving hall and realised I didn't have a hope of finding her with so many people hanging around. I didn't know what to do.

Considering my options, I realised that I should go and stand somewhere like the information desk, after all that would be where she would probably head for once she realised that I apparently wasn't there. Maybe they would be able to give me a sheet of paper that I could use as a sign. Glancing round again I clocked that this was by the exit and just as I was about to head off in this direction, I felt a hand on my arm. 'Excuse me, are you Doctor McCarthy?' I looked up from the hand on my arm into the most extraordinary eyes I have ever seen.

Bates, Bell, Buss, Cooper, Dexter, Langridge, Oakman, Parks, Shaw, Suttle and Thomson

September 1995

Her voice sounded like Moira Steward, who read the news, it was the most English voice I had heard while not listening to the news.

'Mamma Mute?' This produced a peel of laughter that was so filled with delight and joy that I couldn't help laughing as well, not really knowing what was at all funny.

'I see that you are Doctor McCarthy and that you clearly know my daughter Lorena.' I was utterly transfixed by the woman in front of me. She was golden.

She was beautiful. She was indeed petit; she looked like a fragile bird, perfect in every way like a little bird of paradise. Like a perfect white or golden rose. I was utterly spell bound. She reminded me of photos that I had seen of Hollywood actresses from the 1920s and 1930s. After a moment or two, I realised that I was being very rude, standing there and staring at her with my mouth open like a star struck school boy. I hastily lunged for her bags and apologising hurried forwards leading the way to the car. As we drove down the motorway, I apologised for my behaviour, again she laughed with delight and went to some lengths to assure me that I had nothing to apologise for. I snuck a few looks at her as we drove along out of the corner of my eye and there was nothing that I could see, that made her resemble Lorena in any way at all, other than the laugh. After we discussed her flight, my journey to the airport and my busy morning, she said to me,

'Doctor McCarthy, please, do tell me how is my daughter? And what is the matter with her?' I noted that while the warmth in her voice remained, the laughter had gone and was replaced with a very earnest and concerned tone.

'Firstly, please, do not call me Doctor McCarthy, call me James and your daughter has had a nasty shock. She has made a discovery about someone who she thought was a different person and she is having some trouble coming to terms with it. With time though, I think she will be fine.' I silently prayed that this would be so and that this lovely lady would also be fine. There was a moment of awkward silence.

'I see that she has discovered the truth about her grandfather then.' Having already crashed one car and killed my passenger, I had no wish to repeat this action again but the shock of hearing her say that nearly caused me to send us into the drainage ditch at the side of the road. I pulled over to the hard shoulder and stopped the car. Turning and looking at Mamma Mute, I said,

'You know?'

'James, of course, I know. He was my father.'

'Why didn't you tell Lorena?'

'What good would it have done? To tell my children that their grandfather was as good as a mass murderer, who performed sadist experiments on women and children. What would that do to them? What a dreadful secret to have and I am absolutely certain that it would have affected their development and future relationships. No, my father hurt enough people. He was never going to hurt my children,' she said defiantly. As I gazed at her, entirely transfixed by her and the words she spoke, I remembered Lorena's comment about her mother's fierceness and looking at her and the expression on her face, I was in no doubt at all about this point that I had previously dismissed. I suddenly realised something.

'Would you mind very much telling me what your name is? I really don't think that I can keep on calling you Mamma Mute.' She laughed again and my goodness it was a delightful sound.

'James,' she said holding out her hand.

'My name is Eva. I am delighted to meet you. Thank you for being such a lovely friend to my daughter. Lorena is one of the great joys of my life.' We shook hands like people meeting for the first time. I tried to guess her age and wondered if she was called after Eva Perón. With that, I turned back to the steering wheel, put the car into gear, indicated and slowly eased back out into the traffic.

I didn't hang around for the mother and daughter reunion. I felt that this was a very private matter and one that the rest of us did not need to be party to. The fact that Eva already knew the truth and probably much more would help Lorena more than I ever could. I felt very ill-equipped to deal with such a deeply personal matter and decided that other than dropping in to pay my respects tomorrow, I should probably refrain from getting too involved as I was now clearly well and truly out of my depth. Anyway, I had enough of my own patients to deal with.

Later that day, when I was finally home and in my chair, I reflected on Eva's comment about how the knowledge of their grandfather could have destroyed her children's development. I thought long and hard about this. I remembered a young lad called Dan, who was a patient. He was only in his 20s when I got to know him and he was already an alcoholic. He had a fantastic childhood, an only child and very good at sport. He was very keen on martial arts and had progressed on to a very high level in several different disciplines. Just after his 18th birthday, his parents had told him that they loved him more than he could ever know and he had given them what they could never naturally have. They had adopted him when he was just a few months old. His world shattered at that very moment and everything fell apart for him. He couldn't deal with the truth and his lovely and doting parents watched the greatest love in their lives' disintegrate and self-destruct.

By contrast, another patient of mine, who was in her 40s at the time, discovered after her own mother's death that her mother had been adopted. She was distraught that her mother had felt that she couldn't tell the truth and that she had presumably felt ashamed of her circumstances. My patient spent many years researching and trying to make contact with her mother's true relations.

My own mother had her own package of guilt that she carried around with her. As a child she contracted Spanish flu, she was sent to stay with a distant family member so that all of children would not get it, missing her family, she told her aunt that she was better and while still infected went home. Her older and favourite brother caught the flu from her and died within three days. My brother, my parent's first born is called after my mother's best loved and much mourned favourite brother.

The next day, when I turned up at Donatella's for my coffee, I was very surprised to see that Eva and Lorena were both in aprons and serving clients. I looked over their heads at Donatella with a raised eyebrow and catching my look she gave a very melodramatic shrug of the shoulders with her hands in the air. She turned away to make my coffee and I settled down in the corner. Eva came up to me a few moments later with my coffee which she then placed down in front of me.

With a beaming smile she gave me a huge hug and pulled up a chair.

'James, how delightful to see you. I don't think I thanked you for your kindness yesterday. I realise that you are a very busy man and to give up your afternoon like that to come and get me was incredibly generous of you. I do hope that your patients were not too inconvenienced.'

'It was my pleasure. Tell me what is going on?' I gestured towards her apron and Lorena, who was at that point busy chatting to a young family.

'Doctor, I may not have a medical qualification but I have a life time of living with guilt. Lorena sitting at home doing nothing all day other than feeling sorry for herself will help no one. I know that she has had a shock but she needs to pull herself together and get on with life. The damage has now been done and we cannot change the past. However, if we face the future with our eyes open and with love and compassion for each other, maybe we can start to put right some of the wrongs committed by our forefathers.'

'Lorena needs to repay Donatella's enormous kindness and care as do I. So while we are here, enjoying her hospitality, we will help her. All the time that Lorena is sat around, she will not get over her shock but look at her now, she is laughing and smiling.' She looked at her daughter with such affection and pride that I felt a moment of envy for Lorena to be so loved. I looked down at my hands, instantly ashamed of my jealousy.

Eva continued, 'The more active she is, the more she will start to eat again and she will rebuild her strength. She won't be practicing her English sat at home and after all, that was the reason she gave her father and me for coming here. So practice her English is exactly what she will do. It will take her mind off her own worries and she will start to put life back into context again.' She caught the surprised look on my face and reached out, placing the same hand as yesterday on my arm.

'Doctor, I love my daughter so much. She and my husband and our other daughter and son are my entire world. I would do anything for any of them. But just because you love someone does not mean that you can't be firm with them.' I couldn't argue with this logic and to be honest, while I would have taken a different approach to the situation, it was clear that Eva was very much in control of matters and by all accounts was absolutely right. She evidently saw doubt flicker across my face and apparently thinking that I thought she was wrong she explained to me.

'James, did you know that in my country we have the highest instances of Anorexia in the world? Why? Because we, as a nation, are obsessed by how good we look. Buenos Aires has so many plastic surgeons now and people quite literally in some cases give their lives to trying to look good. What a waste and what a futile obsession. We are becoming like The United States as a result and we have more psychiatrists than we do normal doctors or so it seems. There is nothing productive about this. If people worried more about what is on the inside and not on the outside, we wouldn't have this problem in our society. Everyone has problems and issues and mental and emotional scars but why worry about these things when it is far better to acknowledge the situation, learn from it and move on. It is too easy to find someone or something to blame. Each and every one of us has flaws and imperfections but actually these are what make us unique and interesting and set each one of us apart from everyone else. Sometimes, there is no one or nothing to blame. It is just a circumstance. Accept it. Where there is blame attributable, so what, will it really change anything? Will it make you a better person? Will it enrich your life? Probably not. Therefore, I will not tolerate self-pity of any description in my family. We must all learn and move on. Lorena must stop focusing on her hurt and the ensuing insecurities that have arisen from it and be a responsible adult.'

This speech was delivered with such force that I barely had time to register some of the shocking facts that she had just imparted. Little did she know that she had hit so many sensitive spots in my own muddled history and I wondered if this was time for me to examine my own emotional anorexia? I gazed at her reeling from everything she had just said and I wondered if she would be so strong if she wasn't so incredibly beautiful and undeniably gifted. Considering her past, I concluded that she would be.

I saw these two lovely ladies every day when I popped in for a coffee and whenever they could, they would both come over to me and chat. I discovered that Eva's English was so immaculate because she had studied languages at university in Mendoza and had done masters and post graduate studies at both the Sorbonne in Paris and at Oxford University. She spoke not only Spanish, Italian, French, German and English but also Dutch. Purely for recreational reasons she had taught herself Russian and Portuguese. My mind boggled at this as I knew that she had a busy family life and was in charge of running the family beef business.

'How do you have the time?'

'James, an active life and active mind are the best medicine that there is. There is too much self-pity in this world and too many excuses. We must live life while we can. To take pride in oneself makes you want to take pride in all around you and only when you do that can you give life and all components of life, your best. As I see it, it's that simple.' I was awe inspired by this wonderful woman. She didn't patronise and she treated every one as an equal. Her warmth and practical approach to life were so fresh and invigorating that I couldn't help but be caught up in the positivity and practicality of her attitude.

Idly chatting one morning over coffee, I asked her if she admired anyone. It was not the sort of question that I had ever asked anyone before but she was unlike anyone I had ever met before. She looked at me intently before answering. 'Oh, James, so very many people for many different reasons but let me tell you about one, who has affected the lives of so many in my country and who is both hated and admired in equal measures. Her name was Eva Perón.' I had come across this

Eva previously while researching Argentina but it had been a fleeting acquaintance and keen to hear more and possibly more to the point, keen to hear Eva's take on her namesake, I encouraged her to go on.

'Eva Perón, in full Eva Duarte de Perón, née Maria Eva Duarte, also known as Evita, was born in 1919. The second wife of Argentine president, Juan Perón, who, during her husband's first term as president (1946–52), became a powerful unofficial political leader and activist, revered immensely by the lower economic classes.'

'Her parents were not married and her father had a wife and another family, so she and her siblings all struggled financially and the situation was made worse by the death of her father when she was just six years old. At the age of 15, she travelled to Buenos Aires with dreams of pursuing an acting career. She did okay and was a regular on the radio. She attracted the attention of the rising star of the new government, Col Juan Perón and they fell in love marrying two years later. The same year he was ousted by a coup of rival army and navy officers and briefly taken into custody. Following his release, Juan entered the presidential race and Eva forever supportive, was active in the campaign. Honestly, James, she knew how to reach out to the people and she won the adulation of the masses, whom she addressed as Los Descamisados "The Shirtless Ones". Juan Perón was elected and took office in June 1946 and credit must be given to Eva for this remarkable feat.'

'She never held any kind of government post but she did act as de facto Minister of Health and Labour, giving generous pay rises to the unions, who in turn showed political support for Perón. You can understand why she was so loved and

Perón so popular. Approximately, 35% of the country's workforce still to this day belongs to a union. Unions really began during Perón's presidency and he went on to build up the general confederation of labour to approximately 6 million members. Government subsidies were cut off to the traditional *Sociedad de Beneficencia* "Aid Society". In turn, making many enemies among the traditional elite, Eva replaced this with her own Eva Perón Foundation, which was endorsed by "voluntary" union and business contributions including substantial cut of the national lottery and other miscellaneous funds. The revenue raised was used to establish thousands of hospitals, schools, orphanages, homes for the aged and many other charitable institutions.

'Eva was predominantly responsible for the passage of the woman suffrage law and formed the peronista feminist party in 1949. She introduced compulsory religious education into all Argentine schools and in 1951 and although dying of cancer at the time she was nominated as vice president. However, the army forced her to withdraw her candidacy as remember she was bitterly hated by many. Sadly, she died just a few months later, still a young and very beautiful woman. She remained a formidable influence in Argentine politics and to this day is regarded with love and adoration by the masses. Her working-class followers attempted to have her canonised. Her enemies, in an effort to exorcise her as a national symbol of peronism, stole her embalmed body after Juan Perón was overthrown in 1955 and hid it in Italy for some years. In 1971, the military government bowing to peronist demands, returned her remains to her by now exiled widower who was in Madrid. Perón died in office in 1974 in his third term. He had married again and his third wife, Isabel Perón, hoping to win favour with the populace, repatriated Eva's remains and installed them next to her husband in a crypt in the presidential palace. Two years later a new military junta, who were hostile towards Peronism, had both bodies removed. Finally Eva's remains were interred in the Duarte family crypt in a cemetery in Buenos Aires. Only the very wealthy and powerful are laid to rest here. So you see, she divides our country tremendously.' Eva finished her monologue with a sage but sad smile. I sat there bemused and impressed by both the woman before me for her impartial recount of the life of this woman, who had managed to achieve so much in such a short life and against such odds and by the indomitable Eva Perón, who would not let powerful men put her down in an age when women where still fighting for their rights to be heard. Did Eva Perón's roots and ideology put her ahead of her time? Certainly in death, she travelled far more than she could have in her short life! Realising how long I had been entranced by Eva's storytelling, I hurriedly bid her goodbye and spent the next few hours apologising to my patents for keeping them waiting while I failed spectacularly to catch up on time.

I asked "my" Eva some days later, how long she intended to stay here? She paused before answering and looked at her daughter who was cooing over a new mother's baby.

'Lorena is a lot better already. We have talked a lot and we have agreed that she will come back with me to Argentina. I would like to see some old friends of mine from my Oxford days, so we will take a small trip up to see them. We are not ready to go yet though.'

She finished abruptly. I said nothing, secretly relieved that my new friends were not abandoning me yet but panic did grip my heart and desperate to ring every opportunity out of the time we had left together. I completely out of the blue and to my own utter incredulity uttered,

'May I invite you both out for afternoon tea?'

'Oh, James, how incredibly British and what a fabulous idea,' Eva responded clapping her hands together and beaming at me. Glancing across at Lorena, who was yet again actively involved in a conversation she continued,

'On behalf of both of us, we would love to accept, when did you have this in mind for?'

'This Sunday?' The truth was that it hadn't been in my mind at all until I had said it but I was desperate to take every opportunity to spend time with this duo now that the time together had a limit on it.

'I will collect you both at 2.00 pm on Sunday and we can go for a drive in the countryside and a little walk to find a tea room for a lovely spot of tea.' I ignored the fact that I didn't like cakes and sweet things but as this was probably something that they would not enjoy at home it might be a nice experience for them.

Bates, Bell, Buss, Cooper, Dexter, Langridge, Oakman, Parks and Thomson

Late September 1995

As per our arrangement, I collected the ladies at the agreed time, both of whom wore dresses and looked so refreshingly well. Lorena was still on the thin side but she had lost that haunted look and was far less gaunt. Colour was back in her face and the bounce back in her step. I had taken some time and effort with my own appearance and I mused that Lizzie would be impressed.

We drove out into the countryside, past thatched roofed cottages and small villages with impossibly narrow roads and an abundance of antique shops. Some of the names of the villages drew laughs, places such as Cocking and Titty Hill. We ended up taking a walk along the promenade at Bognor Regis, walking past stripy deck chairs and spending time watching the sailing boats and ferries to France sail by. In the distance against the horizon, we could see The Isle of Wight. I explained that Regis is a title given to a place that Royals had historically frequented.

We found an irritatingly small tearoom with wonky mismatched chairs, tables with legs all different lengths so your tea slopped out of the cup every time somebody moved and a proprietor called Sheila with an impossibly large bosom and an annoying tendency to call everyone Love. Still the ladies were delighted by her and hung on her every word, lapping up her stories and to my mind, drivel. The cake stand of cakes, that descended on our table, made me shudder in horror. There were cakes and scones and slices and buns and tarts of all shapes and sizes and brimming with sugar and fat. There were at least four different types of jam on the table along with cream and butter. One could barely move and the misaligned legs made the whole experience a challenge. At least Sheila did provide us with some savoury sandwiches and a linen napkin so not all was lost.

The following Sunday at Eva's request, I accompanied Eva and Lorena on a trip to Arundel Castle. The drive was along the coast road and it took about an hour to get there but we were rewarded with some lovely views out over the sea. Once at the castle, we elected to stroll around the gardens before visiting the Castle itself. To my eye, one garden is pretty interchangeable with another but I was prepared to let myself be swept along by the enthusiasm of the other two.

Eva was most keen on the gardens and armed with a notebook, spent time scribbling down notes. I recalled that she breeds roses and hovered around trying to make useful and helpful suggestions. She smiled at me with pure sweetness and kindness but I felt as if my comments were probably giving away my complete lack of knowledge. As I wandered around rather like a lost cause, a faintly uncomfortable thought crossed my mind, which I wish hadn't. I couldn't help but notice the comparison, though fields apart between Eva's father's professional antics and Eva's fascination with breeding roses. I shook this hurriedly from my mind and was determined to not think of this again as it was a line of speculation which had some uncomfortable conclusions I was sure and I definitely wanted nothing to cloud my thoughts about this wonderful woman.

I found Lorena on a bench and we sat in contented silence watching a water feature splashing away, surrounded by a sea of scarlet and purple flowers, alive with bees and butterflies.

'Mute will be hours yet,' she commented. I looked at her, thinking she was bored but I could see that she was utterly transfixed by a butterfly on a big purple flower.'

'That is a Red Admiral butterfly.'

'How beautiful and lovely, such clear and precise markings; look how the colours contrast so well with the flower.' We carried on sitting in silence and enjoying the peace of the occasion and the warmth of the sun on our faces.

Sometime later, we caught up with Eva. She had found a gardener who worked at the castle and they were in deep conversation about pest control without the use of chemical sprays and pellets.

We moved on to the castle. It was not on a huge scale, rather more like a large country home but it looked very formidable from the outside. Inside was lovely and cool and not too many people were there. I was fascinated to see among all of the family portraits and priceless pieces of furniture, the rosary beads of Mary Queen of Scots there that she took with her to the block. In English History, I had always had a soft spot for this Mary, woefully romantic and easily lead astray by the politically ambitious courtiers around her. She got herself into several scrapes the final of which cost her, her pretty head. We were some hours at the castle and before we left, the ladies insisted on a visit to the gift shop.

To my dismay they emerged some considerable time later with toffee and fudge and shortbread and tea and all sorts of other trinkets to take home to various family members as gifts. Our drive home was punctuated by a delightful feeling of wellbeing by us all. The fields were now being harvested and big wagon wheels of hay dotted the landscape, all waiting to be collected up and stored to provide the cattle with food for the winter. As we drove west towards the glorious sunset which painted the sky in a stunning array of oranges and reds, we all watched in silent awe as this slowly changed to pink and violet. As we all took in the beauty of the scene, a delta formation of what looked like geese flew silhouetted across the glowing sky as if guiding us home.

I think that none of us wanted the day to end and so we collectively decided that a little night cap at the Rose and Crown was called for and sat out under the stars in the beer garden as the warm air gently stirred around us. The twinkling lights in the trees made it feel like an enchanted place. None of us had much to say, yet there was a contented and comfortable silence enjoyed by us all as we each contemplated our own thoughts and memories of the day.

Bates, Bell, Buss, Cooper, Dexter, Langridge and Oakman

October 1995

Several days later, when bringing me my morning coffee at Donatella's, to my surprise Eva asked,

'James, would you mind very much if Lorena and I invited ourselves to dinner with you at your home?' Before I could answer, she continued, 'Donatella really doesn't know anything about what has gone on. I told her that I think Lorena was a bit homesick and maybe lovesick too. I cannot tell that lovely wonderful lady the truth; she would be devastated. However, I need to tell Lorena the whole history of my father and mother and I would appreciate your support because some parts of it are not pleasant and she needs people around her, who will not judge us. She is very fond of you and you have been a truly wonderful friend to her and now to me. I am sorry to be so blunt and take advantage of your kind nature but not only do I need to conclude this story with my daughter but as you have come so far with us, I would like you to know as well.'

'It would be my pleasure.'

'Good,' she said getting up.

'I will bring the steaks and wine around on Saturday evening.' I started to protest but she said,

'James, to understand Argentinian people, you need to understand our culture; to understand our culture, you must first understand our food.' She smiled and walked away.

I was not used to entertaining and really didn't know what two ladies coming to my home for dinner would expect. I took up the matter with Mrs Miller at the first opportunity and asked her for her views and recommendations. It hadn't occurred to me that my predicament could cause so much amusement but before I knew it, Sarah and Mrs Miller were smirking at me the whole time and offering unhelpful, helpful advice. I did ask them not to be so petty and childish about the matter but it seemed to encourage them all the more. When I retired upstairs at the end of a busy Friday surgery, I was pleasantly surprised to discover that the kitchen table which I hadn't seen in years as it was always hidden under a mass of assorted clutter was set and ready with three mismatched chairs set around it. There seemed to be a surprising number of bunches of flowers and equally perplexing, candles everywhere I looked.

Those two must be going soft, how entirely unnecessary. I walked into the bathroom to discover that the toilet roll had been used as an origami experiment and the end of the paper had all be folded back and there was some disgustingly sweet hand soap now in residence on the edge of the sink, not to mention some new frilly hand towels. Goodness only knows what had possessed Mrs M to do that. I wasn't happy about these new additions but I did have to admit that the flat looked clean and tidy and smelt very fresh. Opening the fridge door, looking for something for dinner, I found all sorts of unfamiliar packets and edible goodies not to mention a bottle of champagne chilling in the door. There was an outlandishly large box of chocolates on the side too, which I had just noticed. I now thought I understood the smirks bestowed upon me by Sarah and Mrs M. Talk about crossed wires, I would have to have a very stern chat with them both on Monday morning. The obvious direction of their thoughts made me cringe inwardly and I felt very cross and embarrassed about the whole misunderstanding.

Bates, Bell, Buss, Cooper, Parks, Shaw, Suttle and Thomson

October 1995

Eva and Lorena knocked on my front door, sometime after the allotted 6.00 pm arrival time on Saturday. Both looked utterly charming and entirely different from one another. It was very hard to see the resemblance in them physically; it was only in the gestures, the delighted laughter and the easy grace with which they moved. Both held up their cheeks to me to kiss hello. I was entirely out of my depth with this very demonstrative form of greeting and I didn't really like it at all. I hastily ushered them up the stairs, not entirely comfortable with the new situation that I found myself in.

Eva cried out with delight at the obvious effort that Mrs M had made setting the table and smartening up the kitchen. Lorena disappeared off in the direction of the living room and I found her some minutes later reading through one of my many books.

'You have many books, Doctor, many, many books; they are a part of who you are, I think.'

I looked around my room and it was true there were books crammed into the shelves and where there was no longer any room, piled one on top of the other. Some I hadn't picked up in years and some I had not yet got around to reading and yet looking at them gave me a tremendous sense of who I was and yes, they were a part of me. If I had been a military man, I would have had medals and stripes on my jacket and in the same way, they represent a man's achievements and who he was, my books represented me; they didn't judge me, they didn't argue with me, though some of them did cause me to think and challenged my thoughts but they were like old friends there when I was ready for them, full of interest and ready to go at my pace and always ready to pick up from where we had left off. The thought of being without any of them was simply unbearable. I smiled at Lorena and said, 'Yes, I think you are right.'

Before we could ponder much further, there was a call from the kitchen and as we headed that way, the smell that filled the air made me realise for the first time in a very long time that I was looking forward to eating. Not eating as in the function of survival but eating and savouring lovely and lovingly prepared food. The instant meals that filled my world really were a poor substitute for good food. By the time I walked into the kitchen, my mouth was salivating and I could barely contain my excitement as I surveyed the scene.

'Please, sit down.'

'Lorena, pour the wine, please, *cariño* (darling).' I allowed the comfortable domestic scene to wash over me and realised that had I been a different person, maybe this was something that I could have enjoyed each day with a family of my own. The evening meal when everyone comes together and enjoys the most basic and essential of events while discussing their days together. Something that I am quite sure that many families the length and breadth of the land take for granted every single day and think nothing of how simple but important such a ritual is.

Before I knew what was happening, my glass was full and the food was before me. 'How do you know how I like my steak? You didn't even ask. I usually have it medium.'

'Not this steak, you don't, James, eat it and then you can tell me after if I am wrong.' Needing no further encouragement, I tucked in with gusto and forgetting any manners I may have once had, indulged myself in the flavours before me. I was lost in my own world of pleasure and it was some moments later that I realised that all conversation had stopped and both women were looking at me. Fearing that I had missed a question, I apologised and said that the food was so fantastic and the steak so tender that I hadn't heard a thing. Eva laughed with delight and told me that she was very happy to see me enjoy the meal. As I allowed the candle light, the feeling of warmth and well-being wash over me and hearing but not taking in any of the gentle female chatter, I took a sip of wine. Eva's throw away comment of the other day came back to me, about being able to understand Argentinians. I needed to first understand their food. I considered this point and decided that to be Argentinian must indeed be a happy thing, the food and wine were the product of something far greater than the simple necessity for food and drink. The irony filtered through the back of my mind about Eva's comments about anorexia in her country. When one has a culture of such rich and nourishing sustenance, how is it possible that it can give rise to such a self-destructive condition?

I protested when I was given dessert, not having a sweet tooth and being disapproving in general of refined sugars and pointless calories. My protests were swept aside and Eva fixed me with a firm stare.

'James, sometimes in life, it is not always about what is good for you. Sometimes you must do things, just because and there is no other reason than that. Now eat!'

How on earth could one so delicate and seemingly fragile be quite so stern, determined and quite frankly at moments such as these, terrifying? She allowed absolutely no room for argument and it didn't cross my mind to even question her. Meekly I picked up my spoon and took a mouthful of a desert which I had no idea what it was. I could feel my eyes grow in surprise as I had never tasted anything so sweet but delightful at the same time.

'*Dulce de leche,*' Eva responded as I looked towards her.

'It means sweet milk.' Lorena giggled. 'Enjoy it while you can because I intend to eat whatever is left, Mute's is the best.' Eva smiled at her daughter with affection and pleasure at this final comment.

I was pushed out of the kitchen while the clearing up was done and the ladies found me some time later in my chair with my eyes closed, listening to the all-powerful and commanding Luciano Pavarotti as I relived the pleasure of the meal. The side lights threw out shadows and as I looked at each lady, one so different from another and yet both so similar, I knew that this was a moment that would live with me for ever. In that moment in time, I had never felt so well and happy and loved and completely at peace.

Bates, Bell, Buss, Cooper, Dexter, Langridge, Lenham, Oakman, Parks, Shaw, Suttle and Thomson

The Same Night in October 1995

After sometime of getting comfortable and non-consequential chat, we all fell into a comfortable silence. Eva took a deep breath and began the remainder of her story that she had promised us both she would tell. As I watched the light play over her features and observed Lorena taking in every word her mother uttered, I felt like I was having an out of body experience as if I wasn't really there but was merely looking on. I reminded myself that to an extent I was there in a supporting role as this story in no way impacted my life and yet so far the story had impacted massively on my world. I was in no respect a part of the story and yet, the story was now a huge part of me.

In her calm and melodic voice, Eva recapped a little about what we already knew about her father, his experimentation on humans and his alliance with Josep Mengele at Auschwitz.

'My father died when I was in my early teens, well, I think he died. Suddenly one day he wasn't there anymore and he never came home. For years I wondered why he didn't want to be with Mamita and me anymore. I often asked Mamita why has he gone? Where was he? Will he come back? She would hug me to her and stroke my hair and kiss me on the top of my head. One day I said to her,

'Mamita, I think you know something about my Father.' She took a very deep breath and taking my hand, she led me outside and we sat down on the small balcony looking out over the street, watching the people come and go. She wasn't a woman of words and showed her tremendous love for me through her actions. She however took hold of my hand and quietly and gently began to talk. She said that no matter what, she regretted nothing, because to do so would mean that she regretted me and that she loved me so much that it sometimes caused her an overwhelming feeling that she couldn't describe but I was the treasure in her life, and I made everything make sense.

'Your father went back to his destiny and where he could repay part of a debt he had.'

'I remember feeling a bit lost and confused but I said nothing and let her take her time and slowly she recounted the following story.' Eva explained how as the war started to draw to a close and it became obvious that the Nazis would be caught and would stand trial, they started to vanish. Such was the chaos that existed that many escaped under the wire and without detection. The Red Cross in an effort to help the needy were so swamped and overwhelmed that many Nazis were able to obtain papers with new identities and effectively disappear via this means. The travel papers issued by the Red Cross were called 10.100s and it is estimated that about 120,000 Nazis escaped with these papers issued principally in Rome and Geneva. The Nazis would then escape by the

Ratline routes through Italy and Spain to many locations including Argentina.

At the same time Jews were trying to get to Palestine via Italy and were often smuggled across the border with escaping members of the SS. It was not uncommon for the Nazi's to mingle with the Jews to avoid detection and this is it seems what happened to Eva's mother. *Now the photo of her made sense,* I thought. *I had mistaken her dark looks for those of a gypsy but in fact she was a Jewish lady, possibly from central Europe or the Eastern Mediterranean.* She was a young girl/woman and Eva's father charmed her and showed her attention and gave her little treats, probably trinkets stolen from other unfortunate Jews. In a flamboyant gesture, he insisted that they marry. Together they escaped with the assistance of the Catholic Church, the Red Cross and with those helping the Jews to flee Europe. From Italy they managed to get to Spain. They crossed over the Pyrenees from France. Here they had to get off the train as the French rail gage is that of the international gage at 4ft 8 inches. In Spain the gage is 5 ft. 5 inches. While they waited at the grand station at a place called Canfranc, the wheels were changed on the train. Canfranc was a well-known crossing point for many escaping Nazis and later on went on to be known as the Titanic of the Mountains as it was an enterprise that was overcapitalised in and used for very few years. From here they carried on to the west coast near Santander and they boarded a ship to Argentina.

Eva's mother never questioned how once arriving on new shores; they were provided with a home and instantly her husband had a respectable job. It seems that she was a very naïve girl, who couldn't read and write and who was very much intimidated and scared of her new husband. On their arrival to Argentina and with their new papers, the little affection that he had shown her vanished and she was expected to keep his house, care to all chores and provide meals of his choice. When they had company, she was ordered to vanish and never speak to visitors. Although her mother would never say, Eva suspected that he beat her mother as he had a violent temper and as hard as she tried, she never remembered her father speaking to or touching her mother at all. Thus the years of coldness and being treated as a servant, probably accompanied with beatings and being kept out of sight carried on.

One day a charming man came to their house and instead of being ordered away, she was instructed to stand before both men and remove her undergarments. Shame and horror filled her but she knew better than to defy her husband. This other man was kind to her and tried to sooth her concerns. He examined her and offered her some reassurance. A procedure was performed which she didn't understand. She was then told to replace her clothing and bring them tea.

The realisation some months later that she was pregnant was one of utter confusion and bewilderment. Her husband was so repulsed by her and her heritage that their marriage had never been consummated and this young woman had no idea what was happening to her body. A midwife was called when she went into labour and after many painful hours, a boy and girl were born. Fernando, a boy, whose dark skin and hair took after his mother and a blond petite girl, Eva, resembled more of her father's looks. Fernando, who was born strong and sturdy but suddenly after a couple of months, following a subsequent visit by this man who had performed the artificial insemination, coming to check up on Mother and babies, Fernando became ill and died. His body was taken from Eva's mother who had spent every moment caring for her babies, never to be seen again. She was heartbroken and distraught and became so frightened that Eva would also be taken from her that she refused to let the baby from her sight.

Eva only knew love as a small child, frequently her father was not at home but away working and her mother doted on her. Her father, when he was around, treated her like a valued treasure. Her obvious intelligence was something that he was very proud of and her beautiful, delicate fair looks were something that delighted him.

Bates, Bell, Buss, Cooper and Dexter

That same night in October 1995 as Eva recounted her story.

One day when she was about ten-years-old, Eva came home from school, asking about the war and flying into a rage her father shouted at her to shut up and striding across the room, he hit her across the face and stormed out. It was the first time in her life that Eva had known anything other than unreserved love. 'My mamita told me that in that moment she vowed that he would not hurt either of us again.'

Apparently a man, who she had seen a number of times when she was out shopping and sitting in the park watching Eva play, one day sat down beside her as she watched Eva on the swings. He didn't say who he was but he said that if ever she was ready to confront her husband's evil past, all she had to do was hang a black cloth from the window for three days. By now, although she had never asked her husband, she had a reasonable idea that her husband was a Nazi and had persecuted many of her kinsmen.

'Do not fear for yourself or your daughter, we will look after you.' With that, he got up and walked away after going up and saying something to Eva.

'Mamita was scared by what he may have said to me and I remember she grabbed my hand and hurried me home.'

'What did he say to you?' Lorena asked. Eva thought for a moment and said,

'I don't really remember, something about the importance of working hard at school.'

'The day after my father hit me, Mamita said that she saw the same man again in the park standing by a tree and smoking and instead of looking away as usual, she walked right up to him, looked him straight in the eye and said that she was ready. When she went home, she discreetly hung the black cloth from the window for three days. Father had left for a work conference and we never saw him again.

'The funny thing I remember that day at school, a foreign man visited our school as he was invited to talk to the class about the war and because of his talk at the school, this prompted me to go home and ask questions as he had set us a project of writing an article interviewing our parents on their memories of the war. It was the same man who spoke to me at the park.

'Mamita said that a newspaper is pushed through her front door several months later, she couldn't understand it all as her reading was still very poor but she recognised the photo of her husband and gathered enough to learn that he was back in Europe and after standing trial was found guilty of genocide and executed. She threw the paper away, wanting no more reminders of her despotic and brutal husband. I think though that she drew some strength and confidence knowing that she was free of him, at least in person.

'Some weeks later, the same man from the park bumped into her and said that she wouldn't be rich but would be looked after, provided she kept quiet about what had happened. She asked him who he was and reluctantly he told her that he was part of the Mossad—the Israeli secret police and it was his job to catch the perpetrators of the crimes against the Jewish people.

'He asked Mamita what she knew about her husband. She told him that she was always too scared to ask her husband anything and anyway he never used to speak to her. Clearly he felt that she was owed an explanation, so he told Mamita the story of her husband's past.

'Apparently, the man, who visited them and performed the artificial insemination on Mamita, was my father's former boss and mentor at Auschwitz. One Josef Mengele, otherwise known as the Angel of Death, Joseph Memling, Rudolph Weiss and Helmut Gregor. Like Father, he had escaped to Argentina and although he had returned back to Europe quite openly on a couple of occasions, he had set up his home in Argentina. He became scared when a former Nazi friend of his, Adolf Eichmann, was kidnapped by the Mossad and taken back to Israel by jet. He took off to Paraguay and with the help of a former Hitler Youth leader, Wolfgang Gerhard, he then moved to Brazil. Indeed the Mossad, where on his tail, but for some reason, they never got him.

'Mengele was neutralised as a Paraguayan citizen by 1959, something that my father considered wholly unnecessary it seems, believing I suspect that he was safe by distance and his marriage.

My father and Mengele were both working on projects involving identical twins. They had both attended the Kaiser Wilhelm Institute of Genetics and Eugenics and were dedicated to the concepts of inheritance and pure race, the "Jewish problem" was at the root of this research. They were also obsessed with learning how to change eye colour. Almost all of the experiments were of no scientific value only an ideological one.

'Father frequently went to join Mengele in Paraguay and together they would work for weeks at a time. Mengele would go from farm to farm, checking animals for TB. He would treat the infected animals and he would also carry out artificial insemination on cows and later on, on women. Farmers loved him as he helped many with their herds. The women folk spoke highly of him as he carried out dental treatments as well as treating varicose veins and other ailments. He always carried bottles of potions or tablets which he would give them, but he always took blood samples from animals and humans a like. Believe it or not, he was heralded as being well-mannered and kindly, sympathetic and obliging to help.

'Then an extraordinary event took place in 1963, in the town of Candido Godoi, in Brazil. Twins started to be born, one in five pregnancies were to twins, most of which were blond-haired and blue-eyed.'

Eva was clearly exhausted by this point and was starting to wrap up her story.

Taking a deep breath she carried on,

'So you see, everyone thinks that I look beautiful but my beauty is nothing to be proud of, if anything it should be despised. I am the result of some failed sadistic experiment born out of a sick ideology that took from me my non-identical half, who because his looks were not as mine, was put to his death by his own father, if indeed you can call him that.

'Since the day that I found out about my father, I was determined that my looks would not wear me but that I would wear my looks. I would not let my father's sins in any way define who I am.'

Eva concluded her stunning story by turning to her daughter and saying, 'Lorena, my darling, your grandmother was Jewish, which makes me Jewish and that also makes you Jewish. The very people my father tried to eradicate were people such as us. It will give no comfort to the millions who suffered at the hands of men such as him but in a very small way, there is some sweet irony and we must do everything we can, sweetheart, to try to start to put right some of the wrongs of the past, even if it is just to show our fellow men and women love and comfort but above all, we must not let the past define us, we define ourselves.'

Bates, Lenham, Oakman, Parks, Shaw, Suttle and Thomson

It was the early hours of the morning before Eva finished recounting her story. We were all drained and shattered by the experience of what we heard and Eva had at times been very distressed by what she had to tell us. It was almost too much information to process in one go and for weeks after I was thinking about the different facts and details that she told us that night.

I reflected about the little that I knew about the pre-Nazi movement as we understand it today. In the 1920s in America, there was a group which rapidly grew in popularity within a certain class of people. They became known as the Klu Klux Klan. They basically hated everyone who wasn't like they were. They hated Catholics, Jews, Orientals, Southern Europeans and more commonly they are associated with hating Black people. At its peak, the Klu Klux Klan had between 5 and 8 million members including 75 members of Congress. In many places, Catholics were openly denied places in schools, hospitals and Catholic businesses were boycotted. It became a social as well as a political organisation and frighteningly, the KKK was not the most dangerous of the bigoted organisations in existence at the time. A certain Coalition of Academics and Scientists led by one Dr William Robinson from New York stated that people of an inferior nature had no right to be born but once born had no right to propagate their own kind.

This was an idea expanded on in the publication, Heredity and Human Progress, which argued that the surest, simplest and kindest, most humane way of preventing reproduction among those deemed unworthy of the high privilege is a gentle painless culling. After all in their eyes, too many defectives are around due to careless breeding. This gave rise indirectly to the popularity of the science of Eugenics, the science of the cultivation of superior beings. The idea was to produce healthier, stronger and smarter people. However, it started the introduction of restrictive covenants regarding where people could live, enforced deportations, suspension of civil liberties and enforced sterilisation of tens of thousands of people in America.

The "bible" of the negative eugenics was "The Passing of the Great Race" by Madison Grant, a New York lawyer, published in 1916. This set out the thinking that there was only one good race, The Nordics or Northern Europeans, followed by the Alpines and then finally the Mediterranean's. It wanted no dilution of pure genes and was clear in its argument that one "pure" white person was worth two or three people of ethnic or coloured race. The only way to safe guard the "purity" of the gene pool was to adopt the philosophy of sterilisation, mass incarceration and immigration restrictions. To your average white, privileged, educated blue-eyed, blond haired person in society, this made perfect sense, though this view point sadly neglected to consider the contributions to education and the improvement of society by the likes of Plato and the Roman Empire among others. It is now easier to see the links with the increased momentum of the Nazi movement who followed the thinking set out in The Hereditarily Diseased which, along the same lines, claimed that it was utterly foolish to keep peoples of mental incapacity alive, thus assisting with the purification of the race.

So you see, the Nazis deserve all the blame that is laid at their doors but it is worth remembering that these ideas were around long before and we don't have to look far in some cases to come across others for whom we may have tremendous respect and love for only to realise that they too may well hold similar views, though are probably more private about voicing them.

These reflections led me on to contemplation about the Berlin Wall, a 96 mile super structure and phenomenal and equally shocking concrete wall with 300 guard towers that separated East and West Germany. This went up in August 1961 as a way of the Eastern Bloc countries shielding their population from the more "Fascist" elements, conspiring in the West to prevent the will of the people who "wanted" a socialist state. This wall became known as the Iron Curtain and The Wall of Shame and the area around it on the Eastern side was known as the "Death Strip" for obvious reasons which have been well-documented.

This sickening structure came down in November 1989, reuniting the two halves of the city of Berlin. During the years of the wall, over 100,000 people attempted to escape from Eastern Germany and it is estimated that about 5,000 succeeding in escaping over the wall itself. Between 150–200 people died in their attempts, reports are mixed.

What made me think about the Berlin Wall was not the wall itself but the way that after 28 years of segregation, one people became two and once they were reunited, they remained so. I read many accounts of the problems faced by the people of Berlin once the wall was down. In such a short space of time, the two halves had grown so far apart that it will take generations to attempt to reunite their mind-sets.

The rest of the world regarded the tearing down of the wall as heralding the arrival of universal democracy and a bright future to all in the region, leaving behind the dark days of communism. However, the integration problems between East and West Germany cannot be understated. They were the same people but now with different cultures. The West Germans epitomised slick, hardworking, efficiency, where material wealth is a reward for excellence, education and self-improvement. By contrast, the East German peoples had spent years under a communist regime, where the state provided all they required and they were employed regardless of their attributes. In essence, they were given metaphoric begging bowls which the state filled making all equal—a communist ideal, in turn removing their drive and personal pride, replacing it with apathy and listlessness. I do not attempt to be flippant; their conditions were hardly ideal and certainly not desirable but to an extent by providing all they required to survive, their fundamental desire to succeed was quashed, a communist ideal.

Is this also a problem with an over compensating welfare state? In this country, we are well-provided for and the facilities available to all are the envy of the world. However, are there side effects of this which are not so positive? By being given health care, education and housing, are the values of pride and self-respect and self-improvement stolen from certain individuals? Clearly this is not always the case and is probably the minority but where there is evidence of those who have to fight for improvement, there is generally also greater respect for themselves and those around them as well as an appreciation of what they have.

There is no right or wrong way of saying who should benefit and who should not. As for all intents and purposes, an immigrant to this land, I have benefited hugely from all that was on offer to me. My parents left a poor land in the hope of a better future for themselves and their children and certainly we all took advantage of these opportunities but we studied and worked hard. However, it was not a trip to the land of glory where the streets were paved with gold. The Irish as well as several others were discriminated against. In Liverpool, in the 1960s, there were pubs and bars with signs that said "No Irish, Jamaicans or Dogs."

My parents may have suffered from prejudice from others, I don't know; I don't recall much myself other than light-hearted ribbing for being a "Paddy" and I always gave as good as I got. What happens though when you are not so fortunate? You escape to a land in search of a better life and good fortune and you are not welcomed or worse it is not the land you hoped for? Hatred and dissatisfaction are obvious side effects, I suppose.

I wonder about the people who escaped to Argentina, a much bigger and less densely populated country, maybe one could avoid such scenarios? Is there then a danger of not integrating at all? Does one merely take one's home, customs and beliefs with one? There are many stories of the Welsh who immigrated to parts of Patagonia and who to this day still speak Welsh there with whole communities following Welsh customs. Indeed Lorena once told me that The Welsh Black Cake is a renowned sweet delight in those parts. Is this wrong or perfectly acceptable? Are we successfully travelling abroad and adopting the culture of the land we go to or are we taking our baggage with us and in turn does this cause resentment to both parties?

Surely though by bringing alien cultures to foreign lands and generating a cross pollination of cultures and ways of life, we are evolving societies? Had it not been for the Silk Road and ancient trading routes, we would be more insular and poorer for it. An obvious contrary argument to this would be the infliction by white men of their beliefs and structure of society and government to the Aboriginals in Australia. A peaceful people, who for millennia went about their business of survival until white men burst into their world and disrupted and destroyed their rhythm of life, resulting in problems such as alcoholism and a loss of identity in the name of civilisation.

The "pure breed" ideology of the Nazis was on so many levels flawed and as good as impossible to achieve. For example, my mother was an Irish woman, yet if one were to trace back her family tree, she is the descendant of a Spanish blood line, her raven black hair and olive skin were testimony to this. My father had Norse and Scottish ancestors. For anyone who feels a sense of jealousy towards the nations of other lands, who now reside beside them, stop and consider who your forefathers were? Where did they come from? And where did they go to live? One must not forget that an individual is only six times removed from his neighbour. Are we all really so very different and are our differences of outlook more that we are a product of a societal belief?

I have read about people who have under gone extraordinary feats of human endurance and survival. The key and uniting element in their stories has always been that they never lost sight of their goals and never gave up hope. Therefore, we hope for a better future where prejudice and discrimination fade and go but I fear that this is an ideology which is naïve and unobtainable as by nature humans are jealous of what they and others have and will always try to protect their own and given the chance increase it.

I digress from my story but as I near my inevitable demise, I find I am left with more questions than I have answers for. My experiences and musings have left me lost and bewildered and utterly unsure by what I think I know.

Bates, Bell, Buss, Cooper, Dexter, Langridge and Thomson

Later on in October 1995

Before they left, I asked Eva why her mother stayed in Buenos Aires, a two day drive away from Mendoza.

'Believe me, James, I tried so hard to get Mamita to join us; she would have been so happy helping me with my babies but she refused. It was the first time that I can ever remember her standing her ground. She said to me, 'Cariño, you must go and live your life. I am here if you need me and you will always have a home in this apartment but you are married now and I respect you and your husband's space together. I have friends here and I have a comfortable rhythm of my own now. I don't want to lose that but I will miss you every day.'

'What a remarkably sensitive lady your mother was after all that she went through.'

I wondered about my own mother. She was always there; she provided all I ever needed. I remember she would hold my hand and stroke my hair when I went to sleep at night as a child and would tell me wonderful stories about leprechauns and pixies and their antics after a night on the poteen.

I suppose like all children I took my mother very much for granted as I grew up and by the time of my accident, I was so wrapped up in myself that I never considered her at all. She died of lung cancer shortly before I graduated and never knew

Lizzie. Her death barely impacted on my life as I was totally immersed in my own concerns. I recall that Denis was distraught when she died but at the time I assumed that it was his way of detracting attention away from me as the baby of the family who had lost his mum. I didn't consider how my father felt throughout all of this. He was always such a strong figure.

It was a few days after that night that Eva and Lorena went to Oxford to see Eva's old university friends and they were away for about a week. I noticed a change in them both on their return. They both appeared the same but if you looked carefully at their faces, there were subtle changes. Lorena was more reserved as if a small part of her youth and innocence had gone; the ready laughter took slightly more encouragement and Eva looked faintly wearier. Maybe it was the strain of the last few weeks or maybe it was my imagination but I felt sure that the story of that night had changed them both as it had me.

The night before they left, Eva and I went for a short stroll in the dark. We barely spoke at all, we didn't really need to. Whatever had been left unsaid would now not be ever said. Eva enjoyed my company and I had been a support of sorts to her at a time when the past came back to hurt her beloved daughter and for that she would always be grateful to me. We had enjoyed a number of very pleasurable conversations and had connected both intellectually and emotionally.

Both coming from very different worlds and with very different views, yet across the miles the fates had found a way to connect us in the most unlikely of manors. I knew that I would fool myself for some time in the belief that we would meet again but deep down I knew we would never be in each other's company after their departure from this island and so for my part, I just wanted to hold onto the peaceful companionship that this extraordinary lady brought with her. If I could have bottled it up to keep forever, I would have done so.

I think that for her part, Eva had done so much talking of late that the events of the recent and more distant past had sapped her incredible strength and now she was having to face the future, a future of gently breaking to her other two offspring, the reality of their heritage. She had told me previously that her husband knew about her father but not in great detail and he had felt that it didn't matter and had said to her,

'Let's leave the past where it belongs and focus on the future together.' As we strolled along, each of us locked in our own thoughts, I think without realising it at the time, we both drew some kind of reassurance by the presence of the other, knowing that our time together was about to draw to a close and yet knowing that the joy of our brief friendship would stand the test of time and distance. I walked her to Donatella's door and as she put her hand on the door knob, she turned and looked at me.

'James.' I couldn't bear what she was about to say and so cutting across her, I sighed deeply.

'I know, Eva.'

Without waiting to see her inside, I turned on my heels and walked home. I spent a long time at home standing by the mantlepiece staring at my trophy, looking at it for all the answers that I didn't have.

Bates, Bell, Buss and Cooper October

October 25 1995

They would not allow me to drive them to the airport, instead they took a taxi. They came to say goodbye on their way there.

'My dear. James, I couldn't bear to say goodbye to you in a public place, I would have made such a fool of myself. Instead I wanted to thank you for all you have done for my daughter and me and I wanted to see you here in your flat so that I can always remember you, surrounded by your dusty books.' Eva gave me such a firm hug. She then kissed me on both cheeks and took my face in her hands. I had to stoop to this petite figure. She fixed me with such an intense stare from those extraordinary eyes and said,

'James, take care of yourself; remember how you felt eating that steak and apply that passion and joy to live again, you owe it to yourself. Let the pain and jealousy of the past go, learn from it and don't make the same mistakes but look to the future with your eyes open and…live.' She sighed, trying to control emotion.

'I worry for you, my friend, but I hope that you will be strong and take that leap.' She stared very hard into my eyes for moments which went on for hours.

With that she let go of my face and in her familiar manner patted my arm. I slipped into her hand a pathetically small package.

'Open it on the plane.' She smiled at me and said she would and departed for the taxi.

Lorena sobbed on my shoulder rather like she did several weeks ago and like before, she left a large wet tear soaked patch on my shoulder. I waved until the taxi disappeared around the corner and then found I could not stop waving. To my dismay and complete surprise, I discovered that tears were streaming down my face and suddenly I realised that they would not stop. It was some hours later when I was back in my room, surrounded by my old friends, my books, all of whom were waiting for me when I was ready that I got my emotions back under control. I had cried for the departure of two women from my life, who had in such a short space of time brought so much into my world. I cried for the loss of the excitement and affection, the companionship and stimulation. I cried for the loss of my Lizzie, I cried for the loss of my youth and happiness, the loss of who I thought I was. To my surprise I cried for the lost opportunity of a happy relationship with my brother, Denis, and finally I cried for my own self-imposed isolation. The time and opportunities now lost and with no option to retrieve. I looked up at the now empty space on the mantel piece where my trophy had rested for so many years and knew that although it didn't feel like it at the time, I had done the right thing and taken a step towards letting the past go.

May you have the hindsight to know where you've been, the foresight to know where you're going and the insight to know when you're going too far. Travel blessing.

Bates, Parks, Shaw, Suttle and Thomson

The intervening years from 1995 till the present.

We kept in touch over the years. Eva and Lorena were fantastic correspondents and the monthly letters were several pages with photos included. It would take me some time to read each letter and then I would always go back and read it again. My letters to them were sparse by comparison as I didn't really have much to say. Every letter from Eva finished with the same question.

'James, have you put the past to one side yet? Are you looking forwards with your eyes open?'

I realised after trying to follow her advice for some months that I never would change. Old habits die hard and I was comfortable with my set ways and not willing to try to be a version of the former me. As the months rolled into years, details faded from my day to day life and all rolled into one but I never forgot the happiness and sense of being alive that those few short months which Lorena and Eva brought to my world. The closest I came again was whenever I got one of their letters, I would feel my heart rate go up and feel a tingle of joy and anticipation about what they would have to say in their monthly missive.

I did try once to recreate the steak dinner and went to a reasonably expensive restaurant with an excellent reputation for their steak. However, it was a failure on all levels. The waiter was most attentive and excellent at his job but there was no atmosphere and the meat was chewy and bland. I gave up on the meal half-way through and while assuring the waiter that the food was fine and nothing was the matter, I could not wait to get out and back to my own space. I vowed never again to try to recreate any of those magical moments other than in my mind. Leave the past behind and move on to the future.

After they left on the odd Sunday when I would find myself at a loose end, I would take myself off to a local park or gardens. I suppose I was trying to connect with Eva across the miles through her love of plants and flowers. I started to read different articles in the Sunday newspaper supplements about blights that were affecting certain species of plants or research done into preventing the spread of disease in plants and trees, fantastic blooms that were the result cross pollination, plants with medicinal qualities, the effects of planting certain plants to ward off pests to other plants and so on. I would religiously cut out these articles and post them to Eva for her interest. I took to carrying a camera with me and photographing plants and landscapes and sending the photos with my irregular letters. Eva never failed to comment and was delighted by my efforts and would tell me at length the problems she was encountering with her roses and I would in turn try to find solutions.

More than once I took myself off to the gardens run by the Royal Horticulture Society at Wisley and also to Kew both of which I was able to obtain a fantastic amount of information from. I enjoyed my visits to Wisley and delighted in their herb gardens with the strong smells not dissimilar to apothecary potions. One blisteringly hot Sunday, while sat on a bench in the pine tree section, the wind was blowing in the tree tops. I leaned back and closed my eyes as the heat had made me sleepy and I could hear the trees calling my name over and over again. I must have nodded off because when I came to, I saw Eva and Lorena pointing at me and laughing. I blinked my eyes a few times, surprised but delighted to see them. Slowly they faded into unfamiliar faces of young children who were in stitches to see me asleep on a bench. Glaring at them, I got up and stormed off.

I enjoyed the South American plant section there and imagined that by seeing the plants native to their world, I was in some small way connecting with my two friends. Sometimes, I would take the train to the nearby city of Chichester and walk round the Bishops-gate gardens by the Cathedral and then onto the lovely Priory Park. In the summer there were often archaeological digs on the Roman ruins which would hold my interest for a moment or two. If I felt very energetic, I would walk up to the grounds of the old Victorian psychiatric hospital where the very forward thinking Dr Harold Kidd had encouraged the patients outside and into physical activity, producing marvellous results. I would wander around the grounds there and you could see that in its heyday the gardens, park and orchards had been spectacular.

On a couple of occasions I boldly took the train to Brighton and went to the gardens at Preston Park. I would sit in among the acer trees and think of my past. The surroundings were disturbingly familiar and yet strange as if I knew the area from someone else's descriptions. I would faithfully document the plants and trees I had seen in my letters to Eva and Lorena. On each of my visits to parks and gardens, I would feel a sense of peace and happiness and would be able to indulge my wish to be close to my two friends as I would be able to imagine their delight at certain flowers and their scents or colours. I would return home, feeling a sense of tranquillity that I had spent an uninterrupted afternoon with my two friends, even if it was just in my imagination.

Bates, Bell, Buss, Cooper, Dexter and Lang

In the days, weeks, months and even years after their departure from my day to day live, I felt a degree of grief and emptiness. I realised that for the few weeks that they were a part of my world, it was as if I had inherited a ready-made family of sorts. The punishing emptiness following their return to their home seemed to mock me, making me acutely aware of what I did not have thanks to Lizzie vacating my life. We had never discussed a family but I suppose I had always assumed that would follow but then I had assumed that our marriage was fine too.

I would catch myself thinking *I'll tell Eva that* or *I wonder what the girls would say if we were to go to that.* The momentary forgetfulness was reprimanded with the crushing realisation that I would not be able to do that. The pain and desolation that followed would at times take my breath away and leave me in a state of hopeless panic.

When I felt like that I would struggle to control my breathing, the walls around me would close in and I'd feel clammy and shaky. The impending sense of being alone for the rest of my life would leave me feeling mournful and scared. My world should not have been that way. I was meant to have a wonderful, happy life surrounded by love and adoration and yet here I was, old before my time, unloved and unprotected.

With time these feelings faded a little but would still come back and were brutal in their attack on me when they did resurface. The path ahead looked so bleak and depressing.

Eva and Lorena frequently encouraged me to visit them. While I was working, I felt I couldn't but when I retired I started to make plans for my trip. A lady called Lorraine tells me that I talked of nothing other than buying an air ticket to go to Mendoza but I knew in my heart then that I would never go and at times in fact I didn't believe her at all as I had no recollection of this in the slightest. It occurs to me as I reflect and I write this that I am a lucky man, which is something that I have never considered myself before now. I have known moments of pure happiness. To my surprise, the moments I now conclude to be the best are not while I was a young man, good looking, academically brilliant, a gifted sportsman (tragically, I now realise rather too late in the day that the very moment in my life that I had always felt robbed of at that cricket match was probably rather larger in my own mind that in the reality of life). I was loved by all and I will admit I did enjoy the adoration that surrounded me growing up; later on I enjoyed being respected, acknowledged and having a position of standing in the village that I practiced general medicine in for many years.

No, the moments that I now reflect upon as being the happiest were the few weeks that I spent with Eva and Lorena. They showed me a side of life that I did not know existed and it is probably only now that I recognise that. Moments of peaceful companionship with a few moments of pure sadness and heart break. It's funny to think that moments of emotional upset can be concluded as moments of happiness even though in themselves there are not. To experience these is to live, not to exist. I realise now that Eva told me this repeatedly but I just did not hear her. Ironic really when you think that I dedicated my life to listening to others speak and tell me what was wrong with them and yet, I was not able to hear what I was told was wrong with me.

The pain and devastation of my broken back, the end of my cricket career and the break down and loss of my Lizzie were not coupled by any kind of happiness; they were all in my eyes at the time terminal events, life's betrayal to me. To protect myself from such pain happening again, I prevented any planned or conscious moments of joy, happiness or intimacy, thinking that by not feeling love or happiness again, I would not be hurt and would therefore be happy. What a waste of a life time of possible experiences. As I contemplate my inevitable demise, maybe I should have done things differently but would that have diminished the pure pleasure of those few weeks? I can honestly say now that a life time of a half-life is a price that I am genuinely happy to have had for the time I spent with those two precious ladies who both managed to capture my heart so totally each in their own way. Regret would be an unbearable price to have paid.

Bates and Bell

November

I get so muddled now and confused and start to fret about details that Lorraine tells me are unimportant, yet they take over my thoughts completely. Have I got enough socks? Where will I get my socks from? I must sort out my papers. In the end I work myself up into such a panic. I forget to take my medication and as a result I have had more than one epileptic fit. It takes me longer and longer to recover from each and I always feel just a little bit weaker than I did before, after each one.

I suffer from dizziness and often feel so sick. Cramp grips my feet and I feel so retched. Sleep eludes me for nights on end and when I do nod off, horrid nasty dreams cram themselves into my head that I wake up confused and bewildered. I now insist on having the light on throughout the night. The panic of what I had seen in my dreams sends my heart racing and I have to spend hours working on controlling my breathing. I feel so tired and so utterly defeated from lack of peace in my mind and no rest. No drugs or medication can save me. However, I am thankful that on such occasions I could think back to the feelings I felt one summer many years ago, when I was surrounded by love and companionship, I was eating something wonderful and I felt at peace. My senses were all alive.

I've started hoping after each fit that I won't wake up again because nothing will change, other than being just a little bit less dignified and in control. As the end becomes nearer and yet is still painfully out of reach, I refute the belief that so many hold that to end it all is an act of cowardice, to end it all rather than to suffer through what is to come is a bit like leaving the last glass of wine in an exception bottle of red. You have enjoyed it tremendously but one glass more will make you feel rotten in the morning. You want it but you know it will punish you. It is a choice that you and you alone can make. A glass of wine is rather insignificant in the broader context of life and yet to my mind, it sums up the situation exactly. Yet your most precious possession is life and you are not allowed in the eyes of the law to voluntarily call time. Surely to do so in the correct circumstances is undeniably brave and our basic human right? I hope that while I still can, that I will have the presence of mind and the courage to determine when I wish to bow out with as much dignity as I can muster.

When I close my eyes and concentrate, I remember that we would talk about going horseback riding in the hills through the vineyards. If I closed my eyes, I would be able to feel the sun on my face and hear the bees and insects in the wild flowers around us. The streams would be running fast from the melt water that came down from the majestic mountains that framed the backdrop of our surroundings and I would look up to the skies and see the famous birds of prey soaring overhead. I was surrounded by excited female chatter and laughter and I would feel complete and utter peace and happiness and know in that moment that I was in my spiritual home with those who I loved best. The aroma of the meat cooking over the fire and the satisfying richness of the red full bodied wine added to the pleasure of the moment. This was my moment of salvation, a moment that offered me sanctuary from my circumstances and was where I knew I truly belonged. Where the future held no fear for me and where I was enveloped in love and security. The colours were clear and bright and the images precise, there was complete clarity. There was no fear or confusion, no lost identity or departed memories, where the sun shone on me and where I had succeeded in reaching complete fulfilment and happiness. I needed nothing else from life.

Donde hay amor, hay dolor – A Spanish proverb 'Where there is love, there is pain.'

Lorraine

2 December 2016

My name is Lorraine. Mrs Miller is my aunt and has recently retired owing to her age and bad back. She is over 80 now and has cared for Dr James for over four decades. She didn't want to give up but she does have her own health concerns to worry about, still she comes to see Dr James every week to have a cup of tea with him and scold me on my house keeping skills. I have moved back here after many lifetimes away. I worked for many years in Buckinghamshire and met and married more than one entirely unsuitable man. After each divorce, I promised myself that I would never fall victim to the charms of a complete bastard again but low and behold, somehow, I always did. The last one beat me up so badly that I was in hospital for two weeks with multiple bones broken and a collapsed lung. That was over two years ago. I pressed charges and endured threats and the worst psychological abuse I could imagine. I had worked all of my life, firstly as a nurse and carer in an old people's home and then had gone on to specialise in dementia care. Eventually, I ran a dementia home for over 20 years. Lack of funding and scant resources saw the closure of the home about the time of my own troubles.

Dementia is only just starting to get the recognition as a problem that it deserves. There are many kinds of dementia and it is a silent killer. It is measured in stages and each stage will be unique to the individual. The first three stages quite often go undetected by even the nearest and dearest to the dementia sufferers and often this is the problem, by the time the syndrome is recognised, treatment is too little too late. The changes in behaviour are often so slight that it can be that the sufferer can live for years before being diagnosed. It is usually at about stage four that it becomes evident that things are not quite right. There are often subtle changes in personality and forgetfulness. The individual concerned then moves onto Moderately Severe Decline. By now it is more than obvious what is going wrong and they are possibly not able to look after themselves. Simple facts become a struggle; however, they do generally remember who they are and who their loved ones are. Severe decline is when full time care is required; there are marked personality changes such as aggression and anger as well as considerable confusion.

It is at this point that it is generally time to say goodbye to living at home and invest in a care home with qualified professionals. Quite often it is during this stage that the sufferer may pass away due to other conditions such as a stroke or heart attack. If they do not, then the final stage of dementia is Very Severe Decline. By now the sufferer is probably not all that aware of what is happening to them and may have stopped recognising loved ones.

When I met Dr James, he was at about stage five and having read his story it is clear to see that his dementia was more than obvious to him as he displayed many obvious symptoms. I believe, though he has never told me that he probably had vascular dementia. Many brilliant people develop this; it is not hereditary and is caused by a lack of oxygenated blood to the brain. This can be caused by injury and or lifestyle among other reasons. Increasingly, they are saying that a solitary lifestyle, drinking a sustained amount of alcohol, lack of exercise, poor diet and some long term use medications can all contribute to this syndrome. It is the second most common form of dementia after Alzheimer and there is no cure as it is generally a result of years of decline.

Quite rightly for so long, the headlines have all been about cancer but finally people are waking up to the fact that dementia is a much bigger and more prevalent problem than we all thought before.

My return to the village has been a God send. I was so worn out by my own personal struggles domestically, coupled with the never ending fight to protect the dementia care home that I eventually lost. It was sold off by the owners to developers and now has 24 flats built there. The old and infirm have given way yet again to the young and equally needy.

After a couple of months back in the village, I found that I was actually very bored. I had been spending my time visiting friends and family and helping Auntie Maud, Mrs Miller. When she declared that she couldn't manage any more but didn't want to let the doc down, I instantly jumped at the opportunity.

I had been with Auntie Maud several times to help her at the doc's and found him to be a peaceful charming man, who was very earnest but with a dry and cheeky sense of humour. He could be a little stern at times and did not like to be questioned. He told me a bit about the memories he was writing down. It was clear that his dementia was starting to advance quite rapidly and he was losing the power of concentration. He showed me his notepad where his story was written and I could see the advancement of his condition through his deteriorating handwriting to the point that it was becoming barely legible. He was very concerned about Auntie Maud when she told him that she couldn't cope anymore and thanked her most profusely for all that she had done for him over the years. He made her promise that she would always let him know if he could do anything to help her. I watched him as he struggled out of his arm chair, refusing help and after rummaging around in the top drawer of his desk returned with a cheque book. He asked me if I would be kind enough to write it for him and he would sign it. It was a handsome cheque that he gave Auntie Maud and she cried like a baby.

At this point I broached the subject of taking over from Auntie Maud and he seemed very amenable to the arrangement. I suggested that to start with I come in the mornings to help him get up and get breakfast going. Then I could do some jobs and leave out his lunch and then pop back in the afternoon to get his dinner ready and spend some time with him. I had spoken to the two doctors who ran the practice down stairs and they felt that this was a good idea, given my background in dementia care. The time would come when full time nursing was required but we were not there yet, though I knew it wasn't far away. Dr James was more than acutely aware of his own condition and in his own valiant way he was dealing with it as best he could but as it is a condition without a cure and worse, a condition that robs one of knowledge and more recent memories while slowly eroding and shutting down the communication between the brain and the body, no one can successfully care for themselves indefinitely.

I loved the months that I cared for Dr James. He was gruff and a bit tetchy on the surface but with a bit of determination and perseverance, the quick, warm, funny, still interested and interesting intellect bubbled vibrantly even as day by day the lights were dimming.

Routine was very important and we managed to, more or less, keep to it without too many differences of opinion. There were enough people around to stop him wondering off, which he did try to do from time to time and each time he would insist that he was off to Donatella's for a coffee. The café was still there, though Donatella was not. She had passed away some years back and the café was now run by a young English couple who made passable coffee. Every time we went in, Dr James would say,

'Hello. Tell Donatella that I will have my usual.' The young waitress would look at me in embarrassment but I would say,

'Yes and tell her I will have my usual too, please.' I could tell that she dreaded our visits and was entirely uncomfortable with the situation and embarrassed as well. What she didn't realise though was that this was so important in the ongoing care of dementia sufferers, just maintaining a norm, don't argue and just go along with what they say.

I noted that whenever there was a full moon, Dr James was always more agitated and confused; he also suffered very badly with sun downing. This is when the light starts to fade at the end of the day and it affects the dementia sufferer, making them anxious and disorientated. I always tried to be there about an hour before so that I could draw the curtains and put on every light. I would then sit down next to Dr James and talk to him at length about anything. More often than not about his story and fairly soon, I took over the writing of this while he told me what to say. I have tried to avoid noting down too many of the tangents and keep to the story. He would take off in so many different directions when speaking and we would get lost as to what the point in question was. We would then finish our writing and the Dr would insist that I start at the beginning and read him the whole story.

Some nights he would sit there nodding and smiling and other nights he would interrupt and repeat the story to me as if he had the pages in front of him and was reading to me. He was certainly a night owl and I would be there with him till quite late. I didn't mind at all. We would always enjoy a little drink of wine together. I suspected that there were significant gaps in the story as to my mind not all of the segments gelled. I tried to gently probe these gaps, such as Lorena's dramatic improvement on Eva's arrival but it seemed that the doors to these memories and the story were now closed and the keys lost. Often with people, who have dementia, there are windows of memory and the clarity of their recollection is staggering. However, these should not be taken for granted as what is remembered on one occasion will mean little or nothing to the sufferer on a different day. This was very much the case with Dr James. Sometimes I was a little unsure if what he told me was true or not but I discovered that if he got a bit antsy with my questioning, it could be that these points were not entirely what really happened but if he spoke earnestly and with intent then they were.

One day when reading back the early part of his story, he interrupted me,

'No, you've got it all wrong. I did pay in that game for West Sussex against the West Indies, in fact, it was thanks to me that we won. Make sure that you write that down now.' He got very agitated about this, so I neutrally said,

'Oh, silly me, I must have got muddled. Let me just write that down.' Years of experience have taught me that you never argue and try to correct someone who is having a dementia episode. I made a play of letting him tell me word for work what to write down, but as soon as we started, he got confused and stopped speaking. I carried on reading the story to him and when I looked up some minutes later, I noted he had nodded off. I quietly put down the notebook and went into the kitchen to make a cup of tea for him when he woke up. Dehydration can make things so much worse, so constant cups of tea are essential.

I asked him one day which newspaper he wanted that day and with such sadness in his eyes he looked at me and said,

'My dear, if I could read any paper, I would but I no longer can.'

'Well, my question still stands, which paper do you want today that I can read to you?' I would make a point of reading out the crossword clues to him each day and invariably he would know the word in a heartbeat. They say that music is very good for prompting memories and I have seen this for myself. Sadly, Dr James didn't seem interested in music but I always had the radio on in the background and from time to time a song would come on and he would start to sing along.

It wasn't long after this that we had to get the stair lift installed as walking was becoming more and more of an issue and stairs were now more of a hazard than anything. Once a week Lorena and Eva would call via Skype and Face time and Dr James would always put on a tremendous show for them, acting as if everything was usual and that there was nothing wrong at all. It is extraordinary how some dementia sufferers can do this and if you didn't know better you could well be fooled. I could see that they were not and between us we had developed a code sent via emails that I could say things that on the surface were innocent enough but would tell them, if he was tired or if he out of sorts. They were always careful not to talk for too long and were full of stories and amusing tales.

There was an awkward and difficult conversation when in a moment of excitement, Dr James said to them both,

'Just wait a moment and I will get my friends, Eva and Lorena, to come and say hello. You will love them, you really must meet them.' These two wonderful women acted as if nothing was wrong and Eva said,

'That would be lovely, James. We would like that very much.' I can't be sure but I think I saw tears in Lorena's eyes but Eva carried on chatting away passing the moment off as inconsequential.

I suspected that he was starting to palm his medication. I discussed this with the doctors downstairs and we decided that I would have to watch him take each tablet. The sudden increase in fits and his erratic and angry behaviour were all too familiar on this well-trodden route towards decline. He would suddenly become incensed and would be convinced that I had stolen his newspapers or books his aggression would become very difficult to deal with. I would try to pacify him and tell him that I would put the books and papers back but it would take a long time to calm him down and he would then deny that he had ever said anything at all about the matter. He developed familiar phrases which indicated that he was agitated and stressed.

'I have to go to hospital now. I must get downstairs to surgery or I will be late. We have to get to Donatella's or she will run out of my coffee.' What all of these meant was, 'Everything in my world is going wrong and I can't make sense of anything.'

Plans would need to be made soon for me to move in and care for him full time. His walking was now so bad and he was so unsteady on his legs. The weight has started to fall off him and the light within was slowly starting to be extinguished. He would fret and be inconsolable about the most inconsequential of matters. His breathing would become unsteady and broken. Then suddenly he would take a deep breath and close his eyes. Wherever he went in his mind took considerable concentration and focus but all of a sudden his face would relax and a look of blissful happiness would replace his haggard features and his body would lose its tension. He would then sigh and open his eyes. Terrible sadness would then fill his eyes when he realised where he was. I never asked him where or what he saw but the last time I witnessed this change, he turned his eyes to me and as the tears tumbled down his cheeks, he said in a voice of pure determination.

'My dear, we cannot let this continue.' After a moment, he grabbed hold of my hand and looked at me with such fierce determination.

'Promise me,' he said.

'Promise me you will not let opportunities in your life slip away, look to the future with your eyes open.'

10 December 2016

I cannot put into words the sense of loss and pain that I feel. My dear friend, who I knew for relatively so little time and who I grew to love so profoundly is now released from his torment. As a last act of defiance over his body which had robbed him of so much but could not take from him, his spirit, he refused to eat which caused a massive electrolyte imbalance and irregularities with his heartbeat and regardless of all of the supplements, we tried to get him to drink and take in, it was too little too late. His epilepsy, a direct result of his car accident, coupled with the strain on his heart as a result of the lack of food, carried him away. After a violent fit, he never regained consciousness and in the early hours of the morning after being admitted to hospital and acute care, he passed away holding my hand.

I have thought about what I should do and after reading this story to my dear friend to try to help him remember and helping him to write and finish this when it became too difficult for him, I know that while this story was so important to him, he realised through its telling that his anger at his accident and the sense of injustice of being robbed by all that he felt he was worthy of, had made him very bitter and jealous of those who loved him best. This realisation I think caused him much heartache that he had wasted so much emotion on such irrelevant details and that he had missed so many opportunities through his own obstinacy and pettiness.

Therefore, I am going to take his ashes to Mendoza and scatter them there in the corner of a vineyard called "Mabel Ines" that overlooks the majestic snow-capped Andes mountains and where the rich red soil contrasts strongly against the intense blue skies. He may not have made it in person through his own pride, bloody mindedness and stupidity but I'm determined as hell that he will go to the place about which he knew so much and where a girl and her mother live and come from, that so captured his imagination and attention. Women who woke him up and made him feel alive again and maybe then, he will finally be fully at peace.

I remember that we would talk about going horseback riding in the hills through the vineyards. If I closed my eyes, I would be able to feel the sun on my face and hear the bees and insects in the wild flowers around us. The streams would be running fast from the melt water that came down from the majestic mountains that framed the backdrop of our surroundings and I would look up to the skies and see the famous birds of prey soaring overhead. I was surrounded by excited female chatter and laughter and I would feel complete and utter peace and happiness and know in that moment that I was in my spiritual home with those who I loved best. The aroma of the meat cooking over the fire and the satisfying richness of the red full-bodied wine added to the pleasure of the moment. This was my moment; a moment that offered me sanctuary from my circumstances and where I knew I truly belonged.

May the road rise up to meet you
May the wind always be at your back
May the sun shine warm upon your face

and rain fall soft upon your fields
And until we meet again
May God hold you in the palm of His hand

Irish blessing